Ernest F. Schwaab

The Secrets of Canning

a complete exposition of the theory and art of the canning industry

Ernest F. Schwaab

The Secrets of Canning
a complete exposition of the theory and art of the canning industry

ISBN/EAN: 9783337399603

Printed in Europe, USA, Canada, Australia, Japan

Cover: Foto ©Andreas Hilbeck / pixelio.de

More available books at **www.hansebooks.com**

THE SECRETS OF CANNING.

A COMPLETE EXPOSITION

OF THE

THEORY AND ART

OF THE

Canning Industry.

By ERNEST F. SCHWAAB.

BALTIMORE:

JOHN MURPHY & CO.,

1890.

PREFACE.

This book has been published in response to a popular demand for something of the kind. Trade journals, canned goods brokers and supply houses are constantly receiving letters asking for just such a book as we have endeavored to make this. A glance at the "Contents" will show its nature and scope. It is not meant to be a labored, exhaustive treatise, in a literary sense, but a concise and pointed exposition of the machinery and methods employed in modern canning factories. In a word, it is a practical book for canners and those who wish to learn something about the canning business, being written by a man long identified with the canning industry. Heretofore those who desired to learn anything about canning had to pay an exorbitant price for information often so meagre as to be practically useless, and had to find, by long and costly experiment, the information denied them. We call special attention to the "Processes," which are the feature of the book, and the price of the book will be considered small when it is known that a much larger sum is frequently paid for the "Process" on a single fruit or vegetable.

The list of packers of hermetically sealed goods in the United States, contained in the Appendix, makes the book valuable to supply houses, jobbers, brokers and others.

E. F. S.

July 15, 1890.

CONTENTS.

I.

GENERAL REVIEW OF THE CANNING INDUSTRY.

The first authentic information we have in regard to the canning of hermetically sealed goods dates back to the first part of the present century, 1810, when a work was written on the subject by Appert, and published by authority of the French government. Successful experiments had already been made in this direction, but we owe to Appert the discovery and clear exposition of the principles that underlie the beautiful processes of what has grown into one of the most important of modern industries. But conceding to the discoverer of this great industry all the honor we owe him, we must note that there have been so many improvements on his methods that his book is now of little use to the practical canner, and is interesting chiefly as a bit of history. But little progress was made until 1825, when Thos. Kensett and Ezra Daggett obtained a patent from the United States on an improvement in the art of preserving. But we learn that canned goods were packed in New York by

1

Thos. Kensett as early as 1819, in which year he entered into partnership with his father-in-law, Ezra Daggett. The above patent, which bears the autograph signatures of the then President of the United States, James Monroe, the Secretary of State, John Quincy Adams, and the Attorney-General, William Wirt, in its specifications mentions canned goods in hermetically sealed cans and in such a way as to leave us to infer they were not then considered novel. Thos. Kensett is assumed to have learned the art of preserving in England, before emigrating to this country.

We have various records of the art of preserving from 1832, in which year one Philip Jones, a native of Massachusetts, is mentioned as having put up fruit by a particular process. It is not known just what this process was, but it is believed to have been the same as that employed by Appert. We learn of the catching and preserving of fish in 1835, and, although we do not find by what process they were preserved, we believe it was by the use of brine, as at present. At various periods up to 1840 the art of preserving in hermetically sealed packages is mentioned, but it was far from being general, being known to only a few ; the most progress was made between the years 1840 and 1850. Isaac Winslow, of Portland, Me., is supposed to have been the first to pack sugar corn in hermetically sealed cans for sale. His first experiments were made in 1842, and in 1863, twenty-one years later, he obtained from the United States letters patent for his invention. In 1847 general packing began, that is, the importance of the industry was just beginning to manifest itself, and it was this year that

tomatoes were first packed for commercial purposes and
New Jersey was the place. Appert speaks of preserving
the tomato which he calls *love apple*, but it has little or no
commercial significance in his work. From this time the
industry grew rapidly. In 1849, when the gold fever
broke out, canned food came in great demand on account
of its adaptness for transportation, convenient form and
easy preparation. The next few years witnessed a very
rapid increase and the trade showed a healthy develop-
ment: the range of the pack began to widen and to
include fruits, vegetables, oysters and meats; the standard of quality also improved. Maryland soon came to
the front as the recognized leader and centre of this growing industry, with Maine, New York and New Jersey
following. Now, 1890, the canning industry has grown
to immense proportions, numbering about 20,000 factories
in operation, scattered over the broad domain of forty-one
States and Territories. Maryland leads in the number of
factories, followed by Maine, Virginia, New York, New
Jersey, Delaware, California, Illinois, Alaska, Ohio,
Pennsylvania, Iowa, Kansas, Michigan, Missouri, Massachusetts, Nebraska, Oregon, Texas, North Carolina,
Washington, Indiana, Mississippi, South Carolina, Arkansas, Georgia, Florida, Tennessee, Wisconsin, Colorado,
Connecticut, Alabama, Louisiana, Minnesota, West Virginia, Kentucky, New Hampshire, Rhode Island, Da-
kota, Idaho and Utah, in the order of the number of
their factories. These factories give employment in
various capacities to 1,000,000 persons during the canning
season, while those directly and indirectly concerned
amount to 4,000,000; they use the raw material, fruits,

vegetables, etc., produced on 1,500,000 acres of land, thus furnishing a home market for the products of 30,000 farms, giving employment to a vast number of farm laborers, and bringing in to the farmers $25,000,000 for their produce; they transform this raw material into 600,000,000 cans of food worth $48,000,000 in first hands, a food that is nutritious, healthful and in such a form as to be easily and safely transported to the most remote corners of the earth. Our salmon and other fish canning industries employ 3,000 vessels and 25,000 fishermen, while those directly and indirectly interested amount to nearly 300,000. The yearly output of fish alone is 100,000,000 cans, valued at $18,000,000. The factories engaged in canning fish are located principally on the rivers and inlets of California, Oregon, Washington and Alaska, the latter being engaged in packing salmon exclusively, and Maine.

Then comes Maine with her pack of mackerel, lobster and herring-sardines. But few fish are packed outside of these places except on the gulf coast of Florida, Alabama and Mississippi, where this important industry is just springing up and rapidly developing. The oyster canning industry which has already attained gigantic magnitude, is still growing: engaged in it are 2,000 vessels employing 20,000 hands, while the whole number of persons directly and indirectly concerned will reach nearly 250,000. The annual output of oysters is 75,000,000 cans, valued at about $8,000,000. Then comes the immense and still growing meat canning industry, the centre of which is Chicago. Beef, mutton, tongue, poultry, etc., are packed and shipped to almost every part of the globe. The output of this class of goods in 1889 was worth $22,000,000.

When one takes into consideration the multitude of minor products that find their way to markets in hermetically sealed packages, and add to these the above products, the result is simply marvellous. It is estimated that 350 varieties of fruits, vegetables, fish and meats are packed during their seasons. There is almost no limit to the possibilities of canned food if it is rightly packed and placed before the people. The various methods and improvements which tend to raise the standard of quality and at the same time lower the price are gradually bringing it within the reach of all classes. The rate at which the demand at home and abroad has increased during the last ten years is almost incredible. Canned goods are used in all parts of the world; the exports are continually increasing in spite of the prejudice that exists, especially in foreign countries. Some of this prejudice has doubtless justly resulted from the inferior quality of stuff that has been thrown on the market by unscrupulous packers and dealers, and this can be removed only by removing the cause. But any prejudice against canned goods honestly packed, on the ground that they contain poisonous substances resulting from the chemical action of the contents on the can, is utterly without a just cause. Occasionally some death will be announced through the daily press as having been caused by eating something from a tin can; but announcement is not proof by any means, and certainly there are few who will accept a newspaper's say as necessarily true.

None of the cases of alleged poisoning from eating

canned food have ever been proved, the most of them have been absolutely disproved. We do not know of a single one that has been stated on the authority of a reputable physician. If there existed any such peril to the public the medical journals would certainly have something to say about it, and the people would be aroused to a sense of their danger.

From time to time State chemists have made careful analyses of samples of every kind of American canned food in the market, and in no instance have they found a trace of lead or any other poison. Traces of tin have been found, but tin is not poisonous; every kitchen in the land is well supplied with tin vessels for all sorts of uses and no poisoning ever results. However, the safest course is to use outside-soldered cans exclusively, and we advise this by all means as being the best method for overcoming prejudice abroad. Bismarck, in his recent remarks on the subject of American canned goods, showed that there existed in Germany a very decided sentiment against these goods on account of the inside-soldered cans. Our packers who wish to get a good foothold in the desirable market that Germany offers, will do well to note the above and follow the example of California packers, who are using outside-soldered cans very largely for this season's pack. The few real cases of illness from eating canned food have resulted from its being spoiled and not from its containing poison, and we believe that in the majority of these cases the spoiling took place after the package was opened and not before. Now, canned food honestly put up by the most approved methods will keep a reasonable length of time, several years—there have been cases where the food has been taken from the can many years after it was packed, just as fresh as when put in—but it is not warranted to keep after the seal is broken, any longer than similar food in its original fresh state. It would not be reasonable to expect otherwise. So the prudent housekeeper will bear this in mind and, if she does not use all the contents of a package when it is opened, take the necessary precaution to keep it fresh. It is advisable that the contents of a tin can, particularly tomatoes or any vegetables, or fruits of a similar acid nature, be taken out as soon as the can is opened.

The tests which canned food has successfully undergone during the past fifteen years is wonderful; only improved health has followed its use, and its keeping qualities have been demonstrated by long expeditions in various parts of the world. Not only has it reached the hottest regions of the tropics but has also gone as near the North Pole as explorers have ever ventured: that taken by Stanley and other explorers into the heart of Africa, and by Greely on his Arctic expedition, was opened just as fresh and sound as when first put up.

The wrappers, scattered all over the world, civilized and uncivilized, are monuments to American enterprise, and tell in a voiceless language the simple story of American progress. Tin cans now decorate native huts remote from civilization, and are sometimes worn by the natives as ornaments.

This kind of food is just the thing for those living in mining and lumbering districts; those who go down to the sea in ships; those who travel in the parching deserts or pathless forests; in fact all who are remote from the centres of supplies. What a boon it must be to these toilers on sea and land to have such delicious, healthful food, while their predecessors of a quarter of a century ago were compelled to subsist largely on dry bread and salt junk.

The beneficial effects of good, ripe, sound fruits, in purifying the system and toning up the general health, especially in certain classes of stomach derangements, are well known and yearly growing in favor with physicians who advise the judicious use of fruits in preference to nauseous drugs much more than they did formerly. In the first-class canned article we have something better than similar goods in their so-called fresh state as usually found in the shops of the grocers, who too often palm off stale, unsound fruit on their customers. Then again, the cost, expense of handling, easy preparation, all speak in favor of the canned article as compared with the raw material. But probably the best argument of all in favor of this kind of food is that it can be had in all seasons and in places where the fresh food cannot be obtained.

We are so accustomed to having this easily digested, healthful food, that we look upon it as a matter of course, and often forget what a privilege we enjoy. While the housekeeper of the last generation had to spend the most of her time searching the stalls of the butcher and vegetable dealer and the shop of the grocer for her daily supplies, and seeing to it that they were properly prepared for the table, the housekeeper of to-day can get all these of the first quality, fine flavor, requiring little or no further preparation, and in quantities sufficient to last her any desired length of time so that she need not bother herself again for days or weeks. She can have at hand turtle soup, oysters, meat, fish, vegetables, fruits, all ready to be served at a moment's notice, and need never be caught unprepared by some one dropping in unexpectedly to dinner or supper. All parts of the civilized world vie with each other in preserving their best and offering it at a comparatively trifling cost: Russia sends her caviar; the Mediterranean coast, her sardines; Alaska, her salmon; Canada, her lobster; Maryland, her peaches and oysters; California, her delicious nectarines and fruits of all kinds; and almost every state in the Union, one or more of the fruits or vegetables. A truly great industry! and yet how much greater will it be when the whole world lays aside its silly prejudices and welcomes it with open arms, thus granting its untold millions the privileges which we so greatly enjoy. Various agencies, of which we shall speak later on, are so lowering the price of canned food that it is gradually coming into general consumption, and is fast becoming a staple article instead of the luxury it was a few years ago. Who can tell the good effect that its use, in the place of so much bacon and grease, has had on the health of the people during the past fifteen years? A big stride, you will doubtless say, in the right direction. Yes, but only a step on the long road that will be gone over as sure as the people have the good sense to appreciate a good thing when they see it. No one outside of the trade has an adequate conception of the rapid growth, the immense proportions and great importance of this industry, which is even yet in its infancy, when we think of its possibilities and promise.

Indeed we venture to assert that some of those engaged in it do not fully realize its magnitude and importance, so numerous are its branches and so vast the territory covered. There exists with the general public, a most glaring ignorance of the details of the business on account of the childish and foolish way that managers and so-called "skilled processors" have sought to mystify and hedge in from the vulgar eye their valuable processes; no precious jewel of legend has ever been more zealously or jealously guarded. Even some of the canners themselves do not know as much as they should, having been compelled to pick up here and there by stealth the information denied them by their fellows,—such information is not the most reliable.

We fail to see the reason why one should mystify an operation so simple that a person of ordinary intelligence can learn and efficiently carry it out in a short time, unless it be self-protection. It is quite natural that a man getting $25 a week for comparatively easy work should wish to keep it a profound secret, and veil it in almost sacred mystery; and the more easily the method can be learned, the greater will be the number of those who will learn it, and the greater will be the danger of the "skilled processor" having his salary cut down or losing his place altogether.

But the question may be asked, "why do the proprietors and others interested in the profits of the concern rest content with this state of affairs when they could reduce expenses by being more open and allowing competition to have full sway?" This is certainly a very sensible question, and the ordinary business man, not

interested in this particular industry, will wonder why
there should ever have been a cause for it. Surely no
one will pay a man $25 a week when some one else will
do the work just as well for $15. We must confess that
this question is somewhat puzzling, and the only answer
we have to give is that these people are afraid that some
one with a little capital will learn the secrets and pecuniary advantages of the business and start a rival establishment. So they screen themselves from the view of
these would-be competitors, and to be consistent, as well
as to protect their own interests, they must grant a similar privilege to their employees. Employers and employees combine for a fancied mutual protection. Now
what we propose to do—and we do it without wishing
to antagonize proprietor and processor, or to incur the
ill-will of either—is to place before the public a *bonâ fide*
exposition of the whole of this carefully guarded art;
and in so doing we think we are benefiting the people at
large, and even those who may think we are interfering
with and injuring their business. The sooner any industry or profession is freed from mystery and narrow-
minded policy, the sooner it will find favor with all
enlightened people, and these are the ones who make the
desirable patrons. The moment it shrinks from investi-
gation and hides itself, it forfeits somewhat of the public
confidence and support. No legitimate calling can enjoy
robust health and do the public the most good, so long
as it is handicapped by arbitrary restrictions. If the
methods be of such a nature as to admit of a patent, then
let them be patented, but let the people know all about
them just the same. The more knowledge is dissemi-

nated and restrictions are removed, the more smoothly will the two great economic laws of supply and demand work, to the greatest profit to mankind. Even patents, granting the exclusive use of certain methods or machines to inventors, are advisable solely because men have not yet attained that state of angelic goodness, wherein they are willing to spend their time and means perfecting inventions for the good of their fellows. The processor, if he is a good one, need not fear, for there will always be a demand for an efficient workman at a reasonable salary, so long as the business is conducted on business principles. There are doubtless men in the canning business who agree with us, and will say that we have taken the right position, but very few of these will venture to give an expression of their opinions outside of their association meetings.

Again, we are borne out in what we say by facts: in no part of the country has the business developed more rapidly and surely than in the West, where there is a freer interchange of ideas than elsewhere, and nowhere does it stand on a surer footing.

The various Associations have done much toward eliminating the above-mentioned and other objectionable features, but there is a vast amount of work yet to be done in this direction. The work of the Association should not stop at proposing, discussing and adopting measures that directly concern its individual members, or the Association as a whole, and no one else. This is all very good, but there is something else equally important. It must be admitted that there still exists considerable prejudice among certain classes of people against the use of canned goods, from a real or fancied want of cleanliness in their preparation, and nothing will so quickly kill this prejudice as being always ready and willing to show visitors through one's factory and explain details, thus demonstrating the cleanliness of the various processes and the consequent purity of the food that is being offered to the public. In this way there will be an increased demand for this kind of food, that is, if your material and processes are what they should be. A poor product will inevitably bring disaster in the end. It is perfectly natural that people should wish to know something about the preparation and composition of the food they are eating, and in the present case it is to the interest of all parties concerned that they should know. If canned goods are what they should be, and people are made aware of their value as a food, the demand would be very much greater than it is.

But this principle of secrecy manifestly does not afford the desired protection, if by protection we mean preventing the establishing of new factories, for they are springing up North, South and West. If these are managed by men who have not a sufficient knowledge of the business, and who might be enlightened, then they are not putting first-class goods on the market and are thus doing more damage than good. Again, if there should ever come a time when there is danger of a glut in the market, and consequent loss of profits, men will still continue to rush into the business under the delusion that there is still money in it, when they would stay out of it if they knew the real state of affairs. But happily, this stage has not been reached, for there has always been and still is a demand for a first-class article at a good price. The prediction of some that the birth of so many factories South and Southwest would flood the market and cut off profits have proven false, for business has steadily increased and the market never had a healthier tone than now. The reason is that the growth of the popular taste for this kind of food has kept pace with the production. The best way to quicken this pace is to keep the market well supplied with good, sound, well-packed goods—there cannot be too many of this class—and this will also drive out the ignorant and careless packers whose output does so much mischief. Let *quality* not *quantity* be the packer's watchword. And this quality must be presented in a certain form to suit the tastes of buyers, which some may think capricious, but it must be remembered that they buy such goods only as suit their customers. For example: Peas may be ever so fresh and well packed, yet if they are not properly assorted, but have large and small all mixed, they will not please the fastidious consumer and consequently will not command the highest price from the buyer; peaches may be models in color and flavor and packed in standard syrup, yet if they are chopped up into pieces of all shapes and sizes they will not sell as standards. The standards of the various goods (which we give elsewhere) are the result of long experience and are based on demand, and no packer can safely ignore or neglect them. Of course it is absolutely necessary that good material be used, without which, the standard article will be impossible. The superintendent cannot be too careful about the raw material that comes into his place, especially let it be sound and fresh; and if fruit, neither green nor over-ripe.

Another way to stimulate the demand for canned food is to introduce improved machinery and more economical methods, thus reducing the cost of production and consequently the price to the consumer. The history of this great industry shows that this reduction in cost has gone hand in hand with improvement in product. The price has been still further reduced by the invention of labor-saving machinery for making tin cans, these being the wrappers commonly used in preference to glass jars, which are too expensive and require too much care in handling. The wrapper is an important item, as it is ultimately paid for by the consumer, and hence no food inclosed in costly wrappers can come into general use. When we remember that there are in the U. S. can-making establishments that turn out from 100,000 to 250,000 cans per day, and that these cans are the best and lowest-priced in the market, we may form some idea of the vast influence they exert toward cheapening canned food and increasing consumption. The duty of one cent, as recently proposed in Congress by the McKinley Bill, in addition to the already existing duty of one cent per pound on tin plate used in making cans would add about $3,500,000 to the cost of cans that will be used for a year's packing. As the average price per case of the vegetables and fruits most used by the masses is about $1.75, it is quite probable that about 1,750,000 cases less would be consumed, as the consumers, most of whom are working people, would not be likely to take all this money from the purchasing of other eatables which they look upon as necessaries. We are glad to say that this iniquitous Bill, which seeks to add to the already fabulous wealth of the sheet iron manufacturer under the pretence of protecting American tin, has been laid over and we sincerely trust that it will be killed. But this is only one example of the way our national and State legislators cripple our industries by interfering with the natural laws governing them, of which laws they are too often ignorant or, what is still worse, ignore them.

Having dwelt at some length on the means of increasing the demand for canned goods it may be well to say something about the agencies at work tending to decrease this demand and inflict serious injury on the whole industry. The first that comes to mind is the practice of putting on the can a bogus label stating that it was packed in some famous region, contains a first-class, standard quality of goods, etc., thus totally misleading the public as to the true facts of the case. A large packer or wholesale jobber will contract with a number of small concerns for goods to be delivered without labels, then adorn all these alike—good, bad and indifferent—with the same bogus label proclaiming to the world that they were put up by some fictitious firm in the renowned fruit regions of California or elsewhere. Some grocers do the same thing. These small packers have no reputation at stake, since their names are not on the cans, and so they are not likely to turn out a first-class article, the chief motive being to furnish as cheap an article as possible. This. is not ignorance, or mismanagement, or any of the excusable failings, but downright criminal action, cheating the consumer and damaging the honest packer, and merits the unqualified condemnation of every fair-minded man in the business and the punishment of the law. The industry can ill afford to shoulder the reproach thus cast upon it by such double-dealing, and all honest men interested in it should exert themselves both individually and in their association meetings to ferret out the offenders. Every State should have strict, rigidly-enforced laws against this bogus label practice, and the various Canners' Associations should use their influence in this direction. We cannot lay too much stress on this for if there is any one thing that tends more than anything else to kill the canning industry it is this abominable deception. But fruit and vegetable packers are not alone in this; canned beef packers are addicted to the same trickery as appears from a case which recently came under our notice when in London, wherein a retail meat dealer was found guilty of selling for canned mutton a compound consisting almost entirely of beef with just enough mutton grease added to give it a mutton taste. The bogus mutton was traced to Chicago packers. The grocery shops of to-day present a very different appearance from what they did a dozen years ago, having been transformed by beautifully labeled cans into bright, attractive places instead of the sombre, prosaic places they used to be. Some of the shop-keepers spend much time designing pyramids and various geometrical figures, and by a judicious selection of cans of proper sizes and labels of ‧ harmonizing colors they succeed in producing a most pleasing effect and doubtless draw custom. This is all very good, for we admire the beautiful in art as well as in nature, but it would be more effective if the public had implicit faith in the *bona fide* representation of every pretty label. The contents of the package are of far

2

greater consequence than the wrapper and should not be sacrificed to dazzling chromos.

We have already spoken of some needed reforms that can be best brought about by the various Canned Goods Associations. Here, as in every other business, "in union there is strength" and every canning centre should have an Association to protect and further its interests, which can be done by concerted action much more surely and effectively than by spasmodic individual effort. If any question should arise effecting the right of any packer or packers to use any particular machine or device; or any company should attempt to collect what may be considered unjust or exorbitant charges; or any question whatever, involving the rights and obligations of the packer, should come up, then it is desirable to make a test case of it and settle it once for all, and the Association can retain the services of eminent counsel at a trifling cost to each of its members. Another question of importance that demands consideration and action is that of the weights of cases of canned goods. The packers and transportation lines should agree upon a fixed, standard weight for cases of each size of can, all goods to be received and charged for on this basis by all lines in all parts of the country. This would obviate much confusion and misunderstanding among consignors, consignees and transportation lines and at the same time save the time usually taken up in weighing.

There is nothing more detrimental to the systematic working of business laws as the want of a definite understanding of mercantile usage. And this brings us to another fault in the canned goods business that calls for a remedy:

the absence of any definite understanding as to how a
dealer, who buys goods under a guarantee against " stained
tins," " swells" or any other fault, shall collect the amount
of his claim in case the goods do not come up to the guarantee—that is whether he should ask payment in cash or
in like goods, or have his choice between the two—when
there is no specific agreement on this point between the
buyer and seller. This question certainly has two sides,
the seller has equal rights with with the buyer, and much
trouble and hard feeling arising from dispute would be
avoided by settling it. An agreement, based on business
custom and the rights of the parties concerned, which
leaves no ground for dispute, would be far preferable to a
legal contest. The law often sacrifices equity to techni-
cality. We would suggest that all claims for faulty
goods should be accompanied by the goods as evidence of
the validity of the claim, otherwise some unscrupulous
jobber might think this a good way to get rid of his goods
at cost when the market is going down. The question as
to when and where liability ceases, and where responsi-
bility rests, in case the goods have changed hands one or
more times and are found defective before the expiration
of the guarantee is an important one. Not very long
since a case, wherein a dealer purchased a lot of canned
corn by sample and refused payment at the stipulated
time on the ground that the goods did not come up to the
sample, was tried before one of our city judges and the
judge's decision showed that the law, or at least his inter-
pretation of it, was at variance with the opinion of those
best acquainted with the usages of the business and the
facts of this particular case. Disputes of this kind had

better be referred for arbitration to a committee of disinterested men engaged in the business. This would save time and expense and at the same time better insure justice.

One of the most damaging things for the canned goods packers is the spasmodic fluctuation in the market, due to over-supply and short supply, alternating with an entire ignorance on the part of packers as to what is the real supply. This uncertainty as to what is the amount of goods on the market is caused largely by "bulls" and "bears" who circulate false reports in order to depress or buoy up the market to suit them. Jobbers are responsible to a great extent for this state of affairs and it will be a blessing to the packer when they change their tactics or get out of the business altogether. The sooner this spirit of speculation and gambling can be rooted out and the business conducted on a square basis and under legitimate regulations, the better.

Still, if the jobber must or will stay, then the best thing is for the packers to put themselves in a position where they can get all their information from reliable sources, and they can do this best by combining and forming Associations. Every packing centre should have its local Association, and all these join in a great National Association, more complete and better united than the one recently formed.

Each of these local concerns should keep an accurate account of the quantity of stuff to be packed by each of its members during the season and inform all the other local concerns through the National Association, and this, coupled with the information as to demand, communicated in like manner will enable the packers to gauge their output accordingly, and not be at the mercy of manipulators and sharpers. This is only one of the many good results to be accomplished by the Association. Exhibits of machinery and methods for the general public would go a great way towards removing prejudice; and the same thing, a little more in detail, for members would give each one an opportunity to profit by the experience of all the rest. It is immediately apparent what an advantage this would be, as each one would probably know some useful point that had escaped the notice of the rest; and meeting on a common plane with common interests at stake, could not fail to discourage narrow-minded policy and engender more liberal views.

Again, the apparent glut that sometimes occurs does not come from the packing of too much goods, but rather from the periodic untimely forcing of these goods on the market. Packers, seemingly forgetting that what they put up in three months is to be gradually consumed through the whole year and not swallowed as soon as it is in the can, are disappointed because there is not a sufficient demand among the consumers and retail dealers to take all their pack off their hands right away, and so they get frightened at the threatening glut and are anxious to get rid of their stock. This is just what the jobbers want and they can now buy up all the stock they need, little above, at, or even below cost; they then have the market in their own hands, can deal out their holdings in lots and at times to suit themselves and often dictate prices. There has been no glut, only a hasty crowding of the market. The jobbers know this and turn it to their advantage.

It frequently happens that a so-called glut in a certain

fruit or vegetable in the fall is followed by a scarcity in
the spring; low prices and loss to the packer, followed
by high prices and loss to the consumer. This deluging
the market through ignorance or carelessness is misleading and disastrous and can be easily avoided.

In the first place, each packer, large or small, should
make his calculations to hold on to a good share of his
output and dispose of it through the year at intervals,
dependent on prices, and should not, therefore, incur any
obligations that would compel him to sacrifice it as soon
as packed, at any price he can get. But if, as seems to be
the case, this is impracticable on account of the great
majority of packers not having the necessary capital, then
the next best thing is to have warehouses established at
convenient points—but be sure they are not controlled by
jobbers—where packers can store their goods, getting
therefor receipts specifying kind and quality. These
warehouses should be so managed as to be in a position to
carry the deposits an indefinite period—to the next season, if need be—make advances on them and deliver
them to the order of the depositors. Such a system
would relieve the market of an excessive supply in the
fall, prevent a scarcity in the spring and at the same time
furnish the needed financial aid to packers. Still, even
with the assistance of warehouses at their command, we
would advise packers to use these chiefly as places to store
their goods and to ask for as few advances as possible, for
in borrowing they are incurring obligations which they
must meet, sooner or later, and are thus putting themselves
in the power of capitalists in a certain degree.

One of the best arguments used against small canneries

is that they have so little capital that they cannot keep
it locked up in idle stock, so their goods must be sold to
the first purchaser who comes along, at whatever figure
he may choose to give. But this difficulty may be over-
come to a very great extent by the system of association
warehouses above mentioned. Large canneries have this
advantage over the small. They can use more efficient
machinery, more economical methods, and thus lessen the
average cost per can on their product, and at the same
time they can better hold on to this product and be more
independent in their attitude toward buyers. Small canneries, on the other hand, have a decided advantage over
large ones in putting up certain classes of delicate perishable fruits and vegetables—for example, peaches and
tomatoes,—which require great care and personal attention on the part of the superintendent lest they become
stale before they are packed into the can and processed.
Manifestly, fruits and vegetables of this class, picked long
before they are mature—as they will have to be if they
are to be shipped to a distance—then roughly handled
over miles of transportation lines, thrown into immense
heaps both before and after they are partly prepared, and
prior to being processed, cannot have the delicious flavor
they would have if picked when mature or nearly so,
carted to a factory near by, carefully handled in small
quantities, processed and sealed up before they have a
chance to grow stale or lose their original flavor. This is
only one of the arguments in favor of many small concerns scattered through the agricultural districts, instead
of a few large ones in the great cities. It does not seem
natural to transport perishable raw material from the

centres of production to the centres of population, manufacture it, then distribute it—a large part returning whence it came—when it can be manufactured just as well or even better, where it is grown, and thus save freight and waste. This is not a parallel case to that of imperishable material, as cotton, which requires in its manufacture much capital, high power, and other considerations usually found in cities and towns. Still, in the canning of more hardy fruits and vegetables—for example, apples and corn—which are not easily bruised, can be packed in large quantities by labor-saving machinery, and where the margin of profit is less, the small factories cannot compete with the large. There is much to be said in favor of both small and large factories —they each have their place and the demand is such that they will each continue to exist in spite of the various tactics employed by the latter to push the former to the wall.

In reference to disposing of his pack, if he does so through a broker, we would advise the packer by all means to confine himself to one broker. The principal reason for this is that when several brokers are offering the same goods for sale there may be a slight difference in the prices asked, which the buyers soon discover, and then the packer, through his brokers, is really competing with his own goods. Even if one broker knows another is offering the same goods and at the same price, he does not know how long this will last, and feels altogether insecure, particularly if it is rumored that the other broker is dropping a trifle in his price in order to effect a sale. In either case the market becomes demoralized; seller and buyer lose their tempers, and the probability of a sale is diminished.

A great deal has been said of late about the purchase on a large scale of canneries throughout the country by English syndicates. There is doubtless some truth in the rumor, though we think Englishmen are too shrewd to believe that they can combine in any way to control the output of canned goods in this country, in the same way they are trying to control breweries and other interests, for the simple reason that if they should attempt any such "trust" to maintain a good margin of profit, the people would see what money there would be in the business, and thousands of small factories would spring up all over the country. It is utterly impossible for any company to get entire control of such a business when a comparatively small capital is needed to embark in it, and the field of operation is so large that factories can be started in almost every county in the Union.

The fact that Englishmen have an eye on this industry is significant, however, as showing that they look upon it as one of the most important industries in the New World, and one in which there is money if they can only find a way to obtain possession.

We have only touched upon some of the most prominent features of this industry, which is so young and yet so great. What may we not reasonably expect of it in the next twenty-five years? The steady increase, improvement and cheapening in transportation facilities, both for the raw material and the manufactured product, is giving it a wonderful impetus, and establishing it over the length and breadth of the land. Maryland, long its home and champion, is gradually losing—not her importance, by any means,—but her preëminence as compared with her sister States, some of whom could doubtless give her valuable "points." California, with her luscious fruits, is enabled by cheaper overland freight rates to compete with the East and West in the great markets of the world, while her geographical position gives her the advantage in the trade with Central and South America, Japan, Australia, and the islands of the Pacific. The population of the New World, already high up in the millions, is increasing at an incredibly rapid rate, and this, together with the various agencies mentioned as being at work increasing the demand for canned goods, insures a bright future to the canning industry. And yet, when we compare imports and exports, the result is far from being satisfactory. Why should we, who have such facilities for both producing the raw material and packing it, import so much of the foreign canned article, and export so little of our own? Certainly no country on the globe grows a greater variety or finer quality of fruits and vegetables than ours; and certainly none has made more progress in the art of preserving. This small demand abroad for American canned goods is doubtless due partly to the unscrupulous methods of some packers, and other causes referred to before; but we think that it is due in a very large measure to the improper means employed for putting our goods on the foreign market, together with the want of any mode of bringing them to the notice of the foreign public.

We believe that if our Canned Goods Associations would turn their attention in this direction and devise some means for systematically advertising our goods abroad they would be amply repaid by the increased demand.

They made a great mistake in not having an exhibit at the recent Paris Exposition, for here was a splendid chance to show Europe the excellence of our product. Again, why were the delegates to the Pan-American Congress allowed to depart without ever having seen inside an American canning factory, or having their attention called to the character of its product? Possibly because they might steal some valuable secret and instruct Central and South Americans in the sacred mysteries of the canning house. These opportunities of bringing a great industry, in its proper light, before the eyes of the world have been lost; but there will soon be another rare opportunity—the World's Fair.

Here will be gathered together representatives and exhibits of all the great industries of the world, and the canning industry should be not a whit behind the rest. The National Canned Goods Association should make it a special point to have a full display of all machines and methods employed in the making of cans and the packing of goods, and omit nothing that may serve to impress upon natives and foreigners the real magnitude and importance of the canning industry.

II.

ESTIMATES.

Estimated Amount and Cost of Complete Plants
of Capacities varying from 2,000 to 20,000 Cans
per Day, with Remarks on Special Machinery,
Size of Buildings and Number of Hands required
to Operate.

We propose to give amount of general machinery
required for the different capacity plants, with cost of
same delivered f. o. b. The estimates given are based on
cash figures, and at figures mentioned can be obtained
from any reputable supply house in the country. In
some cases figures will be at variance, but estimates here
given are based on values.

PLANT No. 1.

ESTIMATED AMOUNT AND COST OF MACHINERY FOR
OUTFIT OF 2,000 CANS CAPACITY PER DAY.

We here figure on open-bath process.

1 16-H. P. Boiler, *complete with all trimmings* and
including proper piping and fittings necessary for
connecting Boiler with Tanks.

28

1 Scalding Tank, diameter 36 in., depth 24 in.

1 Exhaust Tank, diameter 36 in., depth 24 in.

1 Process Tank, diameter 36 in., depth 24 in.

4 Scalding Baskets.

2 Exhaust Crates, 1 tier.

2 Process Crates, 2 tier.

1 Perforated Steam Coil or Cross for Scalding Tank.

1 Perforated Steam Coil or Cross for Exhaust Tank.

1 Perforated Steam Coil or Cross for Process Tank.

1 Crane.

1 30-Gal. Gasoline Tank.

1 Air Pump for Gasoline Tank.

1 Air Gauge for Gasoline Tank.

2 Gasoline Fire Pots.

1 Floor Truck.

4 Capping Steels.

4 Tipping Coppers.

1 Forging Stake.

1 Vise.

1 Thermometer.

1 Platform Scale.

2 Can Tongs.

1 Syrup Gauge.

1 Hammer.

25 Buckets.

6 Capping Trays, 2 ft. x 2 ft.

3 Peeling Tables, 3½ ft. x 8 ft.

1 Packing Table, 3½ ft. x 8 ft.

1 Capping Table, 3 ft. x 8 ft.

Estimated cost of this outfit, delivered f. o. b., $460.50.

Remarks.—The above outfit is especially adapted to
canning fruits, berries and tomatoes, as these do not
require so much processing as the coarser kinds. And
we think that, where the more tender and delicate varieties are canned, the open-bath process is preferable to
closed-top steam kettles. We would recommend in this
case the making of open process tanks of diameter and
depth given above. These tanks can be made by an
ordinary cooper, using for the purpose two-inch stuff of
either well-seasoned pine or oak, and should be made in
a substantial manner. This can be done at the home
factory, and they will be found superior to any kettles
furnished for the same purpose and made of boiler iron,
and also much cheaper.

Manufacturers of canning machinery furnish these
tanks for $10.00 each, which figure is included in our
estimate. They will, however, if the matter is left to
them, furnish boiler iron kettles instead, as on every
kettle of this class which they sell their profit amounts to
$10.00, and for *this reason alone* they advise their use.

In fitting up these tanks for processing, a perforated
coil or cross of $1\frac{1}{4}$-inch pipe is placed in the bottom of
each and connected by means of a T with a $1\frac{1}{4}$-inch feed
pipe on the outside, which is joined to a 2-inch main
supply pipe from boiler. If a coil is used (and we
recommend it in preference to cross) a single coil is sufficient, and is best made as follows: Take two pieces of
pipe of required diameter and of a length somewhat less
than the inside half-circumference of tank ; screw a cap
over one end of each, bend each into a half circle and
screw the open ends on the ends of the horizontal or top of

T in such a manner that the closed ends will come nearly together and form a circle in the plane of the T ; then place the coil, holes having been drilled in it so as to throw the steam toward the centre, in the bottom of tank and pass the stem of T through a hole made for the purpose in the side of tank near the base ; join the base of T by means of an elbow to feed-pipe, which runs vertically upward and connects with the main supply pipe passing overhead from the boiler parallel to line of tanks or kettles. The feed-pipe has a valve to regulate supply of steam. The steam is turned on and forced through feed-pipes into coils and against the caps which force it back through the holes toward the centre of tanks or kettles, thus heating the water-bath.

Where one has a boiler on hand, which perhaps he is using for other purposes, he can very readily see how easily he can fit up a first-class outfit, and thus avoid the purchasing of a boiler and kettles which are the chief items of expense in the ordinary outfit. The other articles mentioned in estimate would probably have to be bought of some manufacturer of canning factory supplies, but not necessarily so.

Perhaps a few explanations in reference to the uses of the various articles mentioned as being needed would be a benefit to those living at a distance from sources of supplies, and in many cases these articles may be bought in a home market. For example, a 16-H. P. boiler is necessary for furnishing steam for heating the water-bath ; pipings and fittings are needed for connecting boiler with tanks or kettles. The length of pipe required depends entirely upon the distance that one intends setting the tanks from the boiler.

Scalding kettles or tanks are used for scalding or blanching those vegetables requiring it. Exhaust kettles or tanks are used for exhausting the cans in order to force the cold air out of them after they have been packed and capped. Process kettles or tanks are for processing or cooking the fruit, vegetables, etc., after the cans have been packed, capped and exhausted. Scalding baskets are of galvanized, heavy wire, holding about one bushel, and are intended for scalding tomatoes so they may be readily peeled. (For vessels used in blanching, see "Processes.") Exhaust crates are made of strap iron, having handles for being hooked to a chain worked by a crane for lowering and hoisting crates containing cans when exhausting, and are one can deep. Process crates are like exhaust crates except that they are two cans deep. Steam coils and crosses have already been explained. Crane is used for handling crates in exhausting and processing. Gasoline tank is for holding oil for supplying fire-pots, and requires piping and fittings. Air pump is for pumping air into this tank and forcing oil to fire pots for generating gas. Air gauge is needed for measuring the pressure of air pumped into the tank. Gasoline fire-pots are used in connection with the above for heating capping steels and tipping coppers. Floor truck is used for handling cans as they come from the process kettles. Capping steels are for capping cans after being packed. Tipping coppers are used for closing the vent after the air has been exhausted from the can, thus hermetically sealing it before going to the process kettle to receive the last cooking. Forging stake, for placing coppers on, preparatory to being dressed for retinning. Vise is used for holding coppers for dressing or filing. Thermometer, for testing the heat of water-bath. Platform scales, for weighing purposes about the factory. Can-tongs, for handling cans when hot. Syrup gauge, for ascertaining the density of syrup in canning fruit. Hammer, for hammering out coppers after being placed on the forging stake. Buckets are used by peelers and packers. Peeling tables are used for peeling purposes. Packing tables, for packing purposes. Capping tables, for holding fire-pots and for capping cans.

A building of two stories, 20 x 45 ft., would be a very suitable one for this outfit. Boiler may be placed either in this building or in a boiler-room adjoining. The first floor can be used for process-room, and the second for the storage of empties and stock. To successfully operate this factory would require sixteen hands, as follows: nine peelers, four packers, one processor, one man as capper and tipper, and one fireman. Much depends on the help, and all slow help should be weeded out. Prices paid for peeling, three cents per bucket; packers, fifty cents to $1 per day; processor, $2.50 to $4 per day; capper and tipper, $2 per day; and one fireman, $1.50. Outside of processor, capper and tipper, the help is composed mostly of women and children, and other unskilled labor. The art of processing, as well as that of capping and tipping, is easily acquired.

PLANT No. 2.

ESTIMATED AMOUNT AND COST OF MACHINERY FOR
OUTFIT OF 2,000 CANS CAPACITY PER DAY.

We here figure on Open-bath Process as before, but the
kettles of this outfit are of boiler-iron, as they are intended to be set in brick and heated by furnace.

1 Cast Iron Scalding Kettle, 60-Gal.
1 Boiler Iron Exhaust Kettle ($\frac{1}{8}$ iron), diameter 36 in.,
   depth 24 in.
1 Boiler Iron Process Kettle, diameter 36 in., depth
   36 in.
4 Scalding Baskets.
2 Exhaust Crates, 1 tier.
2 Process Crates, 2 tier.
3 Sets of Grate Bars.
3 Furnace Doors.
1 Crane.
1 30-Gal. Gasoline Tank.
1 Air Pump for Gasoline Tank.
1 Air Gauge for Gasoline Tank.
2 Gasoline Fire-Pots.
1 Floor Truck.
4 Capping Steels.
4 Tipping Coppers.
1 Forging Stake.
1 Vise.
1 Thermometer.
1 Platform Scale.
2 Can Tongs.

1 Syrup Gauge.

1 Hammer.

25 Buckets.

6 Capping Trays, 2 x 2 ft.

3 Peeling Tables, 3½ x 8 ft.

1 Packing Table, 3½ x 8 ft.

1 Capping Table, 3 x 8 ft.

Estimated cost of this outfit, delivered f. o. b., $246.00.

Remarks. — The above outfit is adapted to canning fruits, berries and tomatoes. It differs from Plant No. 1 only in this respect, that the kettles are of ⅛ boiler iron and are set in brick-work, with furnace for heating the water-bath. Numbers of these outfits are being operated in Maryland, principally for canning tomatoes, but we think the process too slow and unsatisfactory. It requires about 3,000 brick for furnace and chimney. The size building best adapted to this outfit is one of about 20 x 45 ft., one or two stories. The same number of help is required as for Plant No. 1.

PLANT No. 3.

ESTIMATED AMOUNT AND COST OF MACHINERY FOR OUTFIT OF 5,000 CANS CAPACITY PER DAY.

We here figure on Open-bath Process.

1 23-H. P. Boiler, complete with all trimmings, and including proper pipings and fittings necessary for connecting boiler with tanks.

1 Scalding Tank, diameter 36 in., depth 24 in.

1 Exhaust Tank, diameter 36 in., depth 24 in.

2 Process Tanks, diameter 36 in., depth 36 in.

6 Scalding Baskets.

2 Exhaust Crates, 1 tier.

4 Process Crates, 2 tiers.

1 Perforated Steam Coil or Cross for Scalding Tank.

1 Perforated Steam Coil or Cross for Exhaust Tank.

2 Perforated Steam Coils or Crosses for Process Tank.

1 Traveling Hoister.

1 30-Gal. Gasoline Tank.

1 Air Pump.

1 Air Gauge.

4 Fire-Pots.

1 Floor Truck.

6 Capping Steels.

6 Tipping Coppers.

1 Forging Stake.

1 Vise.

1 Thermometer.

1 Platform Scale.

4 Can Tongs.

1 Syrup Gauge.

50 Buckets.

8 Capping Trays, 2 x 2 ft.

5 Peeling Tables, $3\frac{1}{2}$ x 8 ft.

2 Packing Tables, $3\frac{1}{2}$ x 8 ft.

2 Capping Tables, 3 x 8 ft.

Estimated cost of this outfit, delivered f. o. b., $646.25. Above outfit is adapted to canning fruits, berries and tomatoes.

A building of two stories, 30 x 60 ft., will be a very suitable one for this plant. Boiler may be placed either in this room or in a boiler-room adjoining. The first floor can be used for process-room, and the second for the storage of empties and stock. To successfully operate a factory of this capacity, would require twenty hands as peelers, eight packers, one processor, two men capping and tipping, and one fireman.

PLANT No. 4.

Estimated Amount and Cost of Machinery for Outfit of 5,000 Cans Capacity per Day.

We here figure on Closed-Top Steam Process Kettle.

1 23-H. P. Boiler, complete, with all trimmings and including proper pipings and fittings necessary for connecting Boiler with Kettle and Tanks.

1 Scalding Tank, diameter 36 in., depth 24 in.

1 Exhaust Tank, diameter 36 in., depth 24 in.

1 No. 2 Steam Process Kettle (Closed-Top).

6 Scalding Baskets.

2 Exhaust Crates, 1 tier.

2 Process Crates, 4 tier.

1 Perforated Steam Coil or Cross for Scalding Tank.

1 Perforated Steam Coil or Cross for Exhaust Tank.

1 Crane.

1 30-Gal. Gasoline Tank.

1 Air Pump.

1 Air Gauge.

4 Fire-Pots.

1 Floor Truck.

6 Capping Steels.

6 Tipping Coppers.

1 Forging Stake.

1 Vise.
1 Platform Scale.
4 Can Tongs.
1 Syrup Gauge.
50 Buckets.
8 Capping Trays, 2 x 2 ft.
5 Peeling Tables, 3½ x 8 ft.
2 Packing Tables, 3½ x 8 ft.
2 Capping Tables, 3 x 8 ft.
Estimated cost of this outfit, delivered f. o. b., $776.25.

Remarks.—The above outfit is adapted to canning all the various fruits and vegetables, oysters, fish and meats.

For general canning purposes closed-top steam process is necessary, but for canning fruits, berries and tomatoes, or such vegetables as do not require such degree of heat, we recommend in all cases the use of open-top process tanks. However, the closed-top steam kettle will answer for processing fruits, berries and tomatoes, but in using we advise throwing the top back, practically making it open-bath, thus combining both processes in the one kettle.

Same size building and same number of hands needed, as in Plant No. 3.

PLANT No. 5.

ESTIMATED AMOUNT AND COST OF MACHINERY FOR OUTFIT OF 10,000 CANS CAPACITY PER DAY.

We here figure on Open-bath Process.

1 35-H. P. Boiler, complete, with all trimmings and including proper pipings and fittings necessary for connecting Boiler with Tanks.

2 Scalding Tanks, diameter 36 in., depth 24 in.

2 Exhaust Tanks, diameter 36 in., depth 24 in.

3 Process Tanks, diameter 36 in., depth 36 in.

2 Cooling Tanks, diameter 48 in., depth, 28 in.

8 Scalding Baskets.

4 Exhaust Crates, 1 tier.

6 Process Crates, 2 tiers.

2 Perforated Steam Coils or Crosses for Scalding Tank.

2 Perforated Steam Coils or Crosses for Exhaust Tank.

3 Perforated Steam Coils or Crosses for Process Tank.

1 Traveling Hoister.

1 62-Gal. Gasoline Tank.

1 Air Pump.

1 Air Gauge.

6 Gasoline Fire-Pots.

1 Floor Truck.

8 Capping Steels.

8 Tipping Coppers.

1 Forging Stake.

1 Vise.

1 Thermometer.

1 Platform Scale.

4 Can-Tongs.

1 Syrup Gauge.

75 Buckets.

12 Capping Trays, 2 x 2 ft.

7 Peeling Tables, $3\frac{1}{2}$ x 8 ft.

3 Packing Tables, $3\frac{1}{2}$ x 8 ft.

3 Capping Tables, 3 x 8 ft.

Estimated cost of this outfit, delivered f. o. b., $929.50.

The above outfit is adapted to canning fruits, berries and tomatoes. A building of two stories, 30 x 70 ft. would be suited for this capacity outfit. The boiler may be placed in this building or a separate boiler room may be constructed. To operate a factory of this capacity would require about fifty hands.

PLANT No. 6.

ESTIMATED AMOUNT AND COST OF MACHINERY FOR OUTFIT OF 20,000 CANS CAPACITY PER DAY.

We here figure on the Closed-Top Steam Process Kettles.

1 60-H. P. Boiler, complete with all trimmings and including all pipings and fittings necessary for connecting boiler with kettles and tanks.
3 Scalding Tanks, diameter 48 in., depth 28 in.
3 Exhaust Tanks, diameter 48 in., depth 28 in.
3 No. 1 Steam Process Kettles.
3 Perforated Coils or Crosses for Scalding Tank.
3 Perforated Coils or Crosses for Exhaust Tank.
3 Cooling Tanks, diameter 48 in., depth 28 in.
12 Scalding Baskets.
9 Exhaust Crates.
9 No. 1 Process Crates.
1 Traveling Hoister.
1 62-gal. Gasoline Tank.
1 Air Pump.
1 Air Gauge.
8 Gasoline Fire-Pots.
1 Floor Truck.

10 Capping Steels.

10 Tipping Coppers.

1 Forging Stake.

1 Vise.

1 2-ton Scale.

8 Can-Tongs.

1 Syrup Gauge.

100 Buckets.

18 Capping Trays, 2 x 2 ft.

12 Peeling Tables, 3½ x 8 ft.

5 Packing Tables, 3½ x 8 ft.

5 Capping Tables, 3 x 8 ft.

Estimated cost of this outfit delivered f. o. b., $1,963.75.

Remarks.—The above outfit is adapted to canning all fruits, also vegetables, oysters, fish and meats. A building, 30 x 80 ft. would afford ample room for this capacity outfit, and to successfully operate it would require about 80 hands, skilled and unskilled labor.

NOTE.—This outfit completes estimates on plants and covers general machinery. Where packers intend operating larger plants than we have given estimates on they can find out the cost by adding additional horse power, tanks or kettles, also other articles—the proportion can be seen by comparison. We intended giving estimates on larger plants, but it would be a hard matter indeed, to give figures outside of general machinery, so we give a list of the various special machinery which would be absolutely necessary in packing anything in large quantities. Anyone contemplating going into the business will do well to carefully look over this list; he may select such machinery as is specially suited to his purpose. For instance, some packers make a specialty of packing corn; others, corn and tomatoes; fruits and tomatoes; or a diversity of fruits and vegetables; still others pack pumpkins, squash, etc., or peas, tomatoes and fruits. The above require special machinery for packing, and no factory combines all.

Pea Hulling Machine.—This machine is used in all large pea-packing factories. It effectively hulls the pea without bruising or crushing, and has a capacity of 600 bushels of Early Junes, or 1,200 bushels of Marrowfats, per day. Cost, complete, about $1,500.

Rotary Pea Separator.—This machine grades peas of all sizes, and has a capacity of perfectly assorting 600 bushels of peas per day. Cost, complete, about $325. Any capacity, however, can be had, up to 1,200 bushels per day.

Corn Cutting Machine.—Cuts the corn from the cob and, is claimed, does far better work than is done by hand. The capacity is put at from 60 to 80 ears per minute. Cost, complete, about $150.

Corn Silking Machine.—Used for removing the silk, or other refuse, from the corn after it is cut from the cob. Prices vary from $50 to $125, according to capacity.

Corn Steaming and Can Filling Machine.—With this machine the corn, after being cut from the cob, silk and other refuse removed, is thrown into a hopper which feeds it evenly into the steamer, where, by means of conveyor shaft, it is carried through the machine, being cooked by steam, which is applied both directly and indirectly while the corn is in transit to the can filler, which discharges it into the cans with the least possible exposure to the air. The cans are then immediately sealed, retaining all the sweetness and flavor of the corn in its natural state. After this they are placed in the process kettle to complete the cooking process. Capacity of this machine is 12,000 cans per day. Cost about $500.

Can Dipping Machine.—Fills cans or jars with liquid of all kinds and is extensively used by packers of corn for filling cans with brine. Cost about $60. ·

Exhausting Machine, for exhausting vegetables, fruits, etc., in cans or jars. The trays are placed in the machine at one end and are carried by an endless chain through the water-bath at a speed so regulated that when they are delivered at the other end of the machine the cans have had the proper time for exhaust. It is provided with coils for heating the water-bath. This does away with the other methods of exhausting hereafter explained. These machines have a capacity of exhausting 14,000 cans per day. Cost about $200.

Tomato and Pumpkin Filler.—Fills accurately the cans with either tomatoes or pumpkin. Prices vary from $75 to $125.

Pumpkin Peeler.—Peels the pumpkin, does accurate work, and can be regulated to any size. Price, about $50.

Pumpkin Grater.—Grates and prepares the pumpkin for the can.

NOTE.—*The above machines can be operated by either hand or steam power.*

Tomato Scalder, for scalding tomatoes before peeling. Used where large quantities of this vegetable are packed, and can be made by the packer himself. The price, if furnished by manufacturers, is $12.

Apple and Peach Parers, Cocoanut and Pine Apple Graters, Cherry Seeders, Apple Corers and Quarterers, for either steam or hand power, can be had, and prices vary accordingly.

Pea Sieves.—Are used in grading peas, where they are packed in small quantities. The peas are hulled by hand, are then placed on the sieve, which is about 2 x 2 ft., and works over a box. The sieve is made by tacking wire over a frame, the wire used, depending on size of peas, which are usually graded in three sizes, and can be made at the home factory.

Pea Blancher, for blanching the peas after being hulled and separated, and before being packed in the can. This blancher is made of light galvanized iron, with handles, and holds about one bushel. It has perforations for admitting the water in scalding. Price, about $2.50.

Peeling Knives.—These are of heavy, short blade, and cost about $1 per dozen.

The following additional articles will also be necessary: *Corn Cutting Knives,* for cutting corn from the cob in packing small lots; also a stiff *brush* is required for removing the silk from the cob before cutting; *brush* for wiping cans; also *lamps, gasoline, solder and soldering fluid.* Ejectors for raising Water, Rubber Hose, etc.

NOTE.—There are various other labor-saving machines, such as power Capping Machines, Test Tubs, Can Wipers, Labeling Machines, etc., but these are not generally used except in very large establishments.

To operate, special machinery will require in addition to boiler an engine of small H. P., also shafting, belting, &c. Where these machines are operated by hand power a boiler is required only, without furnishing motive power. We have in our estimates figured on gasoline fire-pots, as they are used to a larger extent than any other pot. But we have other kinds on the market equally well adapted and at one-tenth the cost, for where gasoline is used it is necessary to have tank, air pump and air gauge, and these amount to a considerable cost, although gasoline fire-pots can be operated by means of a small tank without air pressure. Gasoline in the hands of inexperienced persons is dangerous, besides adding very materially to the cost of insurance. Various fire-pots are to be had, those burning charcoal as low as $2.50, others from $5.00 to $15.00.

CANS.

It may not be amiss to say here something about the tin can in addition to what we have already said in the General Review, and also give estimates of can-making machinery. Durand who took out his patents in 1810, included " vessels of tin," and was the pioneer in the art of making for hermetically sealed food, vessels that combine lightness, durability and cheapness. Glass and stone packages are so expensive, heavy and easily broken that both their first cost and the expense of subsequent handling at the cannery and. by the transportation lines would add so much to the final price of canned food, and so limit the output, that it could not come into general use.

To form some idea of how the vessel affects the price of the package one has only to go into a grocer's shop and price a certain grade of fruit put up in glass jars and then price the same fruit in tin cans. Durand and his successors by their inventions and improvements in can-making, have done almost as much toward bringing canned goods into common consumption as have Appert and his successors, by their inventions and improvements in the art of preserving. Instead of the old cans made slowly by hand entirely, at the rate of perhaps 100 per day, per man, and costing the packer ten cents apiece, we have now immense establishments that make 250,000 cans per day, better than the old ones, and costing the packer only two cents apiece. Most of this advance, made within the last quarter of a century, has been accomplished by the division of labor and the introduction of system, accuracy and labor-saving machines. But curious enough, although the wrapper has been cheapened so much, the contents have been cheapened still more in proportion, so that while thirty years ago the cost of the can was about one-sixth of the cost of the package, to-day it is about one-fifth, on an average.

The following fixtures are necessary for making cans :

1 Foot Press.

1 Pendulum Press.

1 Pair 3-℔. Top Dies.

1 Pair 3-℔. Cap Dies.

1 Pair 2-℔. Top Dies.

1 Pair 2-℔. Cap Dies.

1 Can Header.

1 Pair Sq. Shears.

1 Pair Bench Shears.

2 Pair Hand Shears.

1 Pair Forming Rolls.

4 Solder Frames and Cylinders, 3-℔.

4 Solder Frames and Cylinders, 2-℔.

1 Solder Mould.

1 Solder Cutter.

1 Fire Pot for Seaming.

3 Floating Machines.

1 62-Gal. Oil Tank.

1 Air Pump.

1 Vise.

1 Anvil.

1 Hammer.

Estimated cost, delivered f. o. b., $440.

The above machinery is adapted to making both 2-℔. and 3-℔. cans, which are the ones mostly used. One box of tin plate will make 270 3-℔. cans, or 370 2-℔. cans. This tin plate costs $4.65 per box. The cost of turning out is $2.06 per hundred for 3-℔. cans, and $1.58 for 2-℔. cans. Packers pay for 3-℔. cans $2.20 to $2.40 per hundred; for 2-℔. $1.70 to $1.90 per hundred.

STANDARD SIZES FOR CANS.

No. 1 Cans, 1-lb.........Diameter $2\frac{4}{}$ in., Height 4 in.

No. 2 " 2-lb......... " $3\frac{7}{16}$ in., " $4\frac{9}{16}$ in.

No. 3 " 3-lb......... " $4\frac{3}{16}$ in., " $4\frac{7}{8}$ in.

No. 6 " 6-lb.........Double the capacity of No. 3.

No. 10 " 1-Gal.......Diameter $6\frac{1}{4}$ in., Height 7 in.

All outside measure at largest part.

NOTE.—There are many superior machine-made cans and some packers prefer them to the hand-made, but we believe that the latter cans give more general satisfaction. The prices are about the same. We would again impress upon the packer the desirability of outside-soldered cans, particularly for the foreign trade.

LABELS.

The labeling of cans is very necessary and no packer can afford to do without it.

There has been much progress made during the last few years in the art of designing and turning out handsome labels, and modern cans are covered with fine specimens of the lithographic art. Many large houses are engaged in the business and employ first-class artists for the special purpose of getting up new designs each season. These attractive labels are among the best paying advertisers of canned goods, and thus play a very important part in the business. Let every packer use the prettiest labels he can find, but let him not use bogus labels nor make any misleading statements on his cans. Prices vary from $1.25 to $3 per thousand, according to the size can.

III.

FRUITS.

General Remarks; Varieties Best Adapted to Canning Purposes; Hints on Cultivation; Prices Paid by Packers.

The subject of fruits is such a comprehensive one that we must confine ourselves to a few general remarks, mainly in reference to the selection, planting and cultivation of kinds that experience has shown to be best suited for canning purposes. The reader who wishes to learn all the details of propagating in the nursery, transplanting, cultivating, treating for diseases and insects, of the numerous varieties of large and small fruits, we would refer to the various books on fruit culture, several of which are thoroughly practical and excellent in every respect.

It is estimated that there are nearly four thousand varieties of fruits under cultivation in different countries ;

4   49

the United States alone growing at least five hundred varieties of standard, well-tested apples, apricots, black-berries, cherries, currants, gooseberries, grapes, nectarines, peaches, pears, plums, quinces, raspberries, strawberries and tropical fruits. Besides these there are many varieties not in favor with the people, some of them new and unknown, and the list is yearly growing. The popularity of fruits is due to several causes. In the first place they are palatable, easily digested and healthful. Then again, their cultivation is such a cleanly, invigorating occupation that thousands of professional men, merchants and others, spend their leisure hours in it, gaining health, pleasure and profit.

The value of the fruit product of the United States for 1889, was as follows : Apples, about $55,000,000 ; peaches, $60,000,000 ; pears, $15,000,000 ; strawberries, $6,000,000 ; grapes, $20,000,000 ; other fruits, $24,000,-000 ; making a total of about $180,000,000. The greater portion of these being perishable, their consumption in the green state is confined to a few months, in some cases to a few weeks of the year ; and so, without some practical means of preserving them, a very large part must necessarily go to waste. The canning process furnishes this means, and now millions of dollars worth of choice fruits are preserved with their natural flavor in cans and sent in convenient packages to all parts of the world, where they are enjoyed continuously every month in the year till a new crop comes. With the constantly improving modes of preserving and shipping fruits, the multiplication of the uses to which they are put ; the decrease of freight rates, and the increase of population and exports, there is no danger that the country will not be able to make use of its enormous and continually increasing yield. In 1889 the exports of canned fruits amounted to $915,341.00 ; imports, $1,042,846.00.

It is impossible to make a list of the varieties of any one fruit that best suit *all* canners ; for soil, climate, the trade to be supplied, and various circumstances, must largely help each canner to decide for himself what varieties are best adapted to his needs. We, however, make some suggestions to guide the packer in making this decision, and also give lists of a few of the varieties that have been tested by experience and found to be reliable. These lists are by no means complete, and doubtless each packer knows of other varieties that answer his purpose just as well as any contained therein.

APPLES.

Red Astrachan, Golden Pippin, Duchess of Oldenburg, Fall Pippin, Gravenstein, Hawthornden, Maiden's Blush, Mangum, St. Lawrence, Baldwin, Buckingham or Queen, Fameuse, Jonathan, King of Tompkins County, Northern Spy, Rambo, Rhode Island Greening, Roxbury Russet, Twenty Ounce, Winesap, Yellow Bellflower.

Remarks.—In addition to the above there are many others. Indeed we may say, in general, that any good cooking apple is a good canning apple, and there are so many of these that one cannot fail to find something to suit him in any section of the country. Apples are the most widely grown of all our fruits : there are many fine specimens north, east, south and west. When cooked

(stewed or roasted) they are healthful, nutritious and palatable, and in many cases of sickness are more desirable
than liver pills or any laxative medicines.   There are but
few varieties that keep well through the winter, especially
in the South, hence the need for canning them.   Good
fruit, well packed, will open in the spring as fresh as
when put up and will make delicious pies.   Nearly every
culturist knows, or thinks he knows, how to plant and
take care of apple trees, but a few hints on this point may
not be out of place.   In the first place he should get his
trees from a reliable nursery, and only such varieties as
are adapted to his climate.   Any fault in the soil, unless
it be very great, may be remedied by planting in the following manner : dig for each tree a hole about $2\frac{1}{2}$ feet
square and $1\frac{1}{2}$ feet deep, half fill with a compost—described below—then fill up with surface soil, which has
been carefully laid aside for the purpose, and plant the
tree.   If the soil be very light the compost above mentioned should be made by mixing the earth with ashes,
stiff loam, etc.; if very stiff, mix the earth with sand, leaf-
mould, etc.; in either case a little lime would be advan-
tageous.   If the soil be naturally rich and mellow, the
large holes and compost are not needed.   To obtain the
best results the trees, particularly when young, should be
mulched, that is, the ground over the roots should be covered with a few inches of straw, leaves, half-decomposed
manure, etc.   This keeps the roots moist during a drought
and prevents them from freezing in winter.   Once a year,
in the early spring before the sap rises, the trees should
have a judicious pruning.   For the first five years after
planting, the soil among the trees should be kept clean

and mellow by growing root crops, such as potatoes, or by simply plowing and cultivating.

Packers pay for this fruit from 25 cents to 50 cents per bushel, delivered.

The preparation of apples for the can requires paring and coring machines, hand or steam power. After paring and coring, the apples are packed as solid as possible in the cans, which are then filled completely with water, wiped and capped: if cold water is used the cans are then exhausted; if boiling-hot water is used they need no exhaust. The cans are then immediately tipped and processed. Apples are packed in 3-lb. and gal. cans. The process we give is for 3-lb. cans—allow double this time for gallon cans. It costs to pack the former about 90 cents per case of 2 doz. cans; the latter, about $3.00 per case.

This fruit is in good demand, and pays to pack.

NOTE.—All canned goods are packed 2 doz. cans in a case, unless otherwise stated.

APRICOTS.

Alberge de Montgamet, Breda, Early Golden, Large Early, Moorpark, Peach, Royal, Saint Ambroise.

Remarks.—The Moorpark is probably best known and most valued. Trees grafted on peach stocks require same soil and treatment as peach trees, while those grafted on plum stocks require a heavier soil. We would remark that the latter are preferable in every way. The fruit is delicate and luscious, resembling the peach very closely in appearance and flavor. California is the great apricot section, and annually ships thousands of cans of this fruit to Chicago, New York and other Eastern Markets.

Prices paid by packers from $1.00 to $1.50 per bushel for choice stock.

The fruit is carefully wiped (not pared), halved, packed as solid as possible, without mashing, in the cans which are then filled with cane sugar syrup as called for, either cold or hot, capped, exhausted or not, as the case requires, wiped, tipped and processed. Apricots are packed in 2½-℔. cans, and cost, to pack, about $2.00 per case for choice fruit; $3.00 for extra fine fruit put up in extra heavy syrup.

Good demand and pay well.

BLACKBERRIES.

Ancient Briton, Kittatinny, New Rochelle or Lawton, Snyder, Taylor's Prolific, Western Triumph.

Remarks.—The last two are comparatively new but very promising, the rest have been tested and are standard. Blackberries succeed in any soil that is moderately moist, but if the soil be poor it should be well covered with stable manure in the fall. Plant the canes about four feet apart, cut them off to about one-half their height, and by pruning keep their height between four and five feet, and do not permit more than two or three shoots to grow. In the late fall cut away the old cane that has borne fruit the previous season. A rail or wire should be stretched along each side of the rows to support the canes. The best results will be obtained from them in cold climates if they are covered in winter with a little earth, this is absolutely necessary for the delicate varieties. Probably the best way to do this is to bend them to the earth up the rows and then plow over them a furrow from each side.

The fruit is very extensively used for canning, and, very healthful.

Packers pay from 4 cents to 6 cents per quart for choice cultivated stock, and for common stock 20 cents per bucket.

In preparing for the can, the berries are spread out on the pealing table, all leaves and refuse removed, packed —without being washed—in the cans which are then filled with cold or hot water, wiped, capped, exhausted or not, as the case requires, tipped and processed. Packed in 2-℔. cans and cost about 90 cents per case to pack.

Not a very safe fruit to put up; margin small.

CHERRIES.

Belle de Choisy, Belle Magnifique, Late Duke, Louis Phillipe, Mayduke, Morello, Donna Maria.

Remarks.—We have given only Duke and Morello varieties as these are the best for canning. The Morello and Donna Maria belong to the latter class, the others, to the former class. They are all most excellent of their kind, but if there is any choice it is probably in favor of Belle de Choisy and Morello.

The Cherry is a luxuriant, hardy tree and will grow in almost any soil, but a dry, deep, mellow, rich soil is the one in which it flourishes and bears the most delicious fruit. Cherries when canned retain their natural flavor to a wonderful degree and are unsurpassed for making pies, dumplings, &c., in winter.

Packers pay 30 cents per gallon for first class stock.

For packing, the fruit should not be thoroughly ripe; it is packed whole in the cans which are then filled with cold or hot syrup, wiped, capped, exhausted or not, tipped and processed. The process given is for choice fruit, white or yellow; for the red, or any of the commoner grades, use water instead of syrup; and fruit intended for pies should be pitted. Cherries are packed in 2-lb. cans at a cost of from $1.10 to $2.00 per case, according to variety. There is good demand for choice fruit at a high price.

CURRANTS.

Cherry, Fay's Prolific, Long Bunched Red, Prince Albert.

Remarks.—The bushes should be planted four feet apart; kept well manured, as they are very great feeders, and well pruned. They are very hardy and will bear for twenty years.

The fruit which is so highly valued on account of its delicious mixture of sweet and acid is preserved in a much better form and with a better flavor by canning than by the ordinary drying process. Prices about same as for cherries. This fruit is prepared for the can in about same way as blackberries. Packed in 2-lb. cans at a cost of about $1.75 per case; not of much commercial importance.

GOOSEBERRIES.

American Seedling, Downing, Houghton's Seedling, Smith's Improved.

Remarks.—The above are all American varieties and suited to our climate. There are several good English varieties, but they are more or less subject to mildew in this country.

The bushes are treated in about same manner as Currant bushes, except that they do not require so much manure.

Everyone knows what delicious pies are made of green gooseberries, and by canning the fruit we can have these the year round.

Prices paid by packers 15 cents to 20 cents per gallon. The process given hereafter, and the directions given above, for other fruits, are a sufficient guide for putting up this fruit. Packed in 2-℔. cans, and cost to pack $1.10 per case. Good demand; fair margin.

GRAPES.

Concord, Isabella, Ives, Monroe, Norton's Virginia, Agawam, Catawba, Delaware, Ionia, Rochester, Duchess, Maxatawney, Rebecca, Lady Washington.

Remarks.—The above are some of the most highly esteemed of our hardy, native grapes. There are many very fine foreign varieties, but these are suited only to a warm climate, as California, which is recognized as one of the foremost grape regions of the world. Grapes are the most healthful of all fruits, but the canned article has not yet come into commercial prominence, probably because the fruit can be obtained a good part of the year in its fresh state. However, they make a delicious dessert when stewed, and as they may be easily kept in cans in this state we see no reason why they should not be canned on a large scale.

Packers pay from $20 to $50 per ton, according to variety and condition. Same preparation as for blackberries. Market for choice stock only.

NECTARINES.

Boston, Early Violet, Elruge, Hardwicke's Seedling, Lord Napier, Pitmaston Orange, Red Roman.

Remarks.—This is a species of peach, and requires same culture, but is so troubled with the curculio that it pays to be cultivated in the open air in but few sections of our country. Middle and Southern California are famous nectarine sections, and the fruit that comes hence, whether fresh or in cans, is about the most luscious of all fruits. Packers pay from 75 cents to $1.50 per bushel for choice stock.

Same preparation as for apricots.

Packed in 2½-℔. cans, and cost to pack about $2.85 per case.

Extra fine fruit in extra heavy syrup $3.50 per case.

Good demand; pay to pack.

PEACHES.

(a) Alexander, Early Rivers, Hale's Early, George the Fourth, Mountain Rose, Crawford's Early, Crawford's

Late, Oldmixon Free, Oldmixon Cling, Stump the World, Smock, Heath Cling.

(*b*) Waterloo, Early Louise, Early York, Foster, Alexander, Crawford's Early, Crawford's Late, Conklin, Oldmixon Free, Smock Free, Hill's Chilli.

Remarks.—Varieties in list (*a*) are those that have been successfully grown South and West, while those in (*b*) have been successful North and East. Besides these there are very many others. While the majority are best adapted to certain localities there are some that have given excellent results throughout the country wherever introduced. Peach canning is one of the most important branches of the canning industry. While any fine flavored peach will do to can, the medium size, yellow, spicy, firm peach is the one most sought after by packers because it brings the best price.

The trees are not so hardy as apple trees, nor so well suited to cold clayey soil or cold climate, nor do they keep their vigor so long, but are planted and cared for in about the same way.

The "yellows," which is supposed to result from improper cultivation, is shown by a yellow foliage, puny fruit, and is contagious. This disease which is spreading rapidly in some sections is justly dreaded by fruit-raisers, and trees should be destroyed when there is any sign of it.

Packers pay from 50 cents to $2.00 per bushel, depending on season, quality and variety.

No article that finds its way to market in hermetically sealed packages affords a better opportunity than do peaches for testing the packer's art. Peaches after being pared or not, and cut into proper sizes, according to grade of goods desired, are filled as solid as possible, without mashing, into the cans which are then filled with syrup, or water and the process completed. They pay well; fancy goods bring extreme prices. They are put up in 3-℔. cans and cost to pack : "Extra," heavy syrup, $2.75 per case; "Standard," $2.00 per case; "Seconds," $1.50; "Pie Fruit," $1.10 per case.

PEARS.

Varieties on Pear Stocks: Bartlett, Clapp's Favorite, Seckle, Doyenné Boussock, Doyenné d' Eté, Lawrence, Beurré d' Angou, Beurré Bosc, Le Conte.

Varieties on Quince Stocks: Duchesse d' Angoulême, Beurré d' Angou, Howell, Louise Bonne de Jersey, Vicar of Winkfield, Beurré Giffard, Brandywine.

Remarks.—The trees should be treated just as apple trees. The fruit when properly canned makes a fine dessert, beautiful to look at and delicious to the taste.

Packers pay from 40 cents to $1.25 per bushel for Bartletts, and for other and inferior varieties from 35 cents to $1.00. Pears are put up in 2-℔. cans and cost to pack from $1.10 to $1.80 per case, according to variety. Good demand; pays to pack.

PINEAPPLE.

This fruit is largely imported from the West Indies. It also comes from the south coast of Florida, where its cultivation is now being extensively carried on; the section of the State best adapted to its cultivation is along the Indian and St. Lucie rivers, Lake Worth, and South along the coast to Key West.

The canning of this fruit is a large and growing industry. Baltimore is the only place where it is packed to any extent.

Packers pay for good, sound fruit, from $6.00 to $9.00 per hundred.

The fruit should be carefully sliced or grated and contain no eyes; cans must be full. We advise a heavier syrup than 10° for fine goods. Packed in 2-℔. cans, and cost to pack about $2.10 per case for "Standard;" and about $3.00 per case for fancy goods with extra heavy syrup and without cores. Fine goods bring fancy prices.

PLUMS.

Coe's Golden Drop, Green Gage, Gellemberg, Imperial Gage, Magnum Bonum, Pond's Seedling, Smith's Orleans.

Remarks.—These grow best in rich, clayey soil, and may be managed in about the same manner as apple trees except that the branches should be regulated to a great extent by pinching off small shoots in summer, instead of too much pruning, in order to prevent gum. They are very liable to be infested with insects, and must be carefully looked after. The canning of this fruit is confined mostly to California, and this branch of the canning industry has grown very much during the past two or three seasons. Packers pay from 75 cents to $1.50 per bushel for good fruit.

This fruit, which should be of good varieties and

nicely packed, is put up in 2-℔. cans and cost to pack
from $1.25 to $1.75 per case. Good demand for fine
fruit, which pays well.

QUINCE.

Angers, Champion, Pear-Shaped, Rea's Seedling.

Remarks.—By care and attention in pruning, the tree
may be made beautiful in appearance and prolific instead
of the unsightly, barren thing it too often is. The fruit
when well cooked has an excellent spicy flavor, and is
highly prized either alone or mixed with other fruit to
give it a flavor ; it is therefore an excellent fruit for canning purposes. Packers pay from 50 cents to $1.00 per
bushel.

Quinces are pared and cored like apples, but are put
up in syrup. They are put up in 2-lb. cans and cost to
pack, $1.40 per case. Pretty good demand and fair mar-
gin of profit.

RASPBERRIES.

American Black Cap, Brandywine, Cuthbert, Gregg,
Miami, Souhegan, Turner, Hudson River, Antwerp.

Remarks.—The canes require same treatment as blackberries, except that they should be kept about a foot
shorter. The canned fruit ranks next to blackberries in
popularity and importance. Packers pay from 15 to 20
cents per gallon.

Raspberries are prepared as other berries already described, but are put up in syrup. Packed in 2-℔. cans and
cost to pack $1.25 per case. Good demand and margin.

STRAWBERRIES.

Duchesse, Kentucky, Monarch of the West, Sharpless, Wilson's Albany, Hoffman.

Remarks.—The transplanting should be done in early spring, as soon as the ground is moderately warm and dry. Place the plants two feet apart in rows two feet apart. They should have plenty of stable manure, if the soil is not naturally rich, be kept moist and clean of weeds and grass by working well with cultivator. It is well to protect them during winter with a light covering of loose straw, hay or half-rotted manure. The plants are quite hardy and are successful in all kinds of soil, though they have yielded best results in a deep, sandy loam. The " Seedling " varieties are not so good for canning.

It is needless to say anything in praise of this fruit, which is so well known and highly prized all over the land. In the canned form it is excellent for many purposes and very popular.

Packers pay for choice berries from 3 cents to 6 cents per quart, delivered.

After having the caps removed, strawberries are prepared in the same manner as raspberries, but we advise a heavier syrup than 10° for extra goods. They are put up in 2-℔. cans and cost, to pack, about $1.20 per case for " Standard," $1.70 for " Extra." They are in good demand and pay well.

WHORTLEBERRIES.

This fruit grows wild throughout the country, in some districts in immense quantities, and is not cultivated.

Packers pay about 20 cents per gallon. They are prepared as blackberries, and put up in 2-℔. cans, at a cost of about $1.25 per case. Good demand; fair margin.

NOTE.—Observe that the above remarks on the cost of packing the various fruits apply to the ordinary standard grades put up in tin cans. Extra fine grades, put up in glass jars and other vessels, with extra heavy syrup, cost considerably more.

----

(2)

PROCESSES.

OPEN-BATH AND CLOSED-TOP STEAM KETTLES.

NOTE.—*Observe* that it is impossible with the open-bath process to get a greater degree of heat than 212° F.; in the closed-top process any degree of heat can be obtained. Remarks as to the merits of the two systems will be found in our estimates on plants. By closed-top bath, dry and moist steam can be used in processing. We recommend the latter, as the dry steam is very liable to impart a burnt taste to the goods unless great skill is used.

Observe the following points in using open-bath process: The kettles or tanks are filled about half-full of water. After lowering crates containing cans in exhausting and processing the time should be taken when the water is at boiling point, 212°, and not before, the required time is then allowed as called for by exhaust and process.

Observe the following points in using closed-top process: After the crates are filled with cans to be processed place them in the kettle three crates deep; fill the kettle up to the upper blow-off pipe, then bolt the lid securely and allow the valve at the upper blow-off to be partly open until the water boils, or the thermometer registers 200° to 212°, then close the valve perfectly tight. The safety valve should be set to blow off at 12 lbs. pressure, which is equivalent to 240°, thus to avoid over-cooking by excessive heat.

APPLES.

"Standard :" Pared and cored, clear in color, cans to be full of fruit, free from decay, put up in water.
Exhaust cans: 5 minutes at 212°.
Open-bath : allow 10 minutes process at 212°.
Closed-bath : allow 3 minutes process at 240°.

APRICOTS.

"Standard :" Cans to be full, fruit to be free from specks and decay, put up in not less than 10° of cold cane-sugar syrup.
Exhaust cans: 5 minutes at 212°.
Open-bath : allow 10 minutes process at 212°.
Closed-bath : allow 3 minutes process at 240°.

BLACKBERRIES.

"Standard :" Cans to cut out not less than two-thirds full after draining; fruit to be sound, put up in cold water.
Exhaust cans: 3 minutes at 212°.
Open-bath : allow 7 minutes process at 212°.
Closed-bath : allow 3 minutes process at 240°.

CHERRIES.

"Standard :" Cans to be full of fruit, free from specks and decay, put up in not less than 10° of cold cane-sugar syrup.
Exhaust cans: 7 minutes at 212°.

5

Open-bath : allow 12 minutes process at 212°.
Closed-bath : allow 4 minutes process at 240°.

CURRANTS.

" Standard : " Cans to be full of ripe fruit, free of specks
and decay, put up in cold water.
Exhaust cans : 7 minutes at 212°.
Open-bath : allow 12 minutes process at 212°.
Closed-bath : allow 4 minutes process at 240°.

GOOSEBERRIES.

" Standard : " Cans to cut out not less than two-thirds
full after draining ; fruit to be unripe and uncapped,
put up in cold water.
Exhaust cans : 7 minutes at 212°.
Open-bath : allow 12 minutes process at 212°.
Closed-bath : allow 4 minutes process at 240°.

GRAPES.

" Standard : " Cans to be full of fruit, free from decay,
put up in cold water.
Exhaust cans 5 minutes at 212°.
Open-bath : allow 12 minutes process at 212°.
Closed-bath : allow 4 minutes process at 240°.

NECTARINES.

" Standard : " Cans to be full of fruit, of good size, cut
in half pieces, put up in not less than 10° of cold
cane-sugar syrup.

Exhaust cans 5 minutes at 212°.

Open-bath: allow 10 minutes process at 212°.

Closed-bath: allow 3 minutes process at 240°.

PEACHES.

"Extra," "Standard," "Second:" Cans to be full of fruit, evenly pared, cut in half pieces, put up in not less than 10° of cold cane-sugar syrup.

"Pie Fruit:" Cans to be full, fruit sound, unpared, cut in half pieces, put up in cold water.

Exhaust cans 5 minutes at 212°.

Open-bath: allow 10 minutes process at 212°.

Closed-bath: allow 4 minutes process at 240°.

PEARS.

"Standard:" Cans full, fruit white and clear, pared, cut in half or quarter pieces, put up in not less than 10° of cold cane-sugar syrup.

Exhaust cans 5 minutes at 212°.

Open-bath: allow 12 minutes process at 212°.

Closed-bath: allow 5 minutes process at 240°.

PINEAPPLE.

"Standard:" Cans to be full, fruit sound and carefully pared, slices laid in evenly, put up in not less than 10° of cold cane-sugar syrup.

Exhaust cans 10 minutes at 212°.

Open-bath: allow 20 minutes process at 212°.

Closed top: allow 8 minutes process at 240°.

PLUMS.

"Standard:" Cans to be full, fruit sound, put up in
water; fine grade, in 10° cane-sugar syrup.
Exhaust 5 minutes at 212°.
Open-bath: allow 12 minutes process at 212°.
Closed-bath: allow 5 minutes process at 240°.

QUINCE.

"Standard:" Cans full of fruit, pared and cored, cut
in half or quarter pieces, put up in not less than 10°
of cold cane-sugar syrup.
Exhaust cans 7 minutes at 212°.
Open-bath: allow 15 minutes process at 212°.
Closed-bath: allow 6 minutes process at 240°.

RASPBERRIES.

"Standard:" Cans to cut out not less than two-thirds
full after draining; fruit to be sound, put up in
not less than 10° of cold cane-sugar syrup.
Exhaust cans 3 minutes at 212°.
Open-bath: allow 6 minutes process at 212°.
Closed-bath: allow 2 minutes process at 240°.

STRAWBERRIES.

"Standard:" Cans to cut out after draining not less than
half full of fruit, which shall be sound, and not of

the varieties known as "seedlings," put up in not less than 10° of cold cane-sugar syrup.

Exhaust 3 minutes at 212°.

Open-bath : allow 6 minutes process at 212°.

Closed-bath : allow 2 minutes process at 240°.

WHORTLEBERRIES.

"Standard :" Cans to be full ; fruit to be sound, put up in cold water.

Exhaust 5 minutes at 212°.

Open-bath : allow 7 minutes process at 212°.

Closed-bath : allow 3 minutes process at 240°.

NOTE.—The manner of preparation of fruits and vegetables for the can is of the greatest importance to every packer of hermetically sealed food. Having dwelt on the evil of putting up inferior goods we trust packers will do all in their power, by concerted action, to crush out this evil. It costs but little more to put up good goods than it does to put up inferior, and the difference in price is vastly in favor of the former ; besides, it creates demand for this already favored food. In packing fruits and berries cans should in all cases be packed as solid and carefully as possible. The term "to cut out," as applied to cans, means simply to contain so much solid matter when opened— hence the necessity of avoiding excessive cooking in the case of some fruits, as strawberries, which go to juice. After the cans are packed they are filled completely with water, or syrup, as called for. Where small quantities are packed (several thousand cans per day) a very good arrangement for filling cans is a tank with spigot attached. It would be well to have two tanks, one containing water, the other syrup of the proper density. The cans are placed on the capping trays, passed under spigot and carefully filled. For larger packs, a dipping machine is better. (See special machinery.)

Observe carefully: The "standard" calls for the cans to be full of fruit, sound, etc., put up in cold water or cold cane-sugar syrup. If this is done it will be necessary to exhaust cans. If, however, the water, or syrup, be boiling hot the cans need not be exhausted but are immediately scaled and processed. But we recommend the exhaust as being the surest method. For heating syrup, a good method would be to have in the tank a coil connected by means of pipe with the boiler.

IV.

VEGETABLES.

(1)

General Remarks; Varieties best adapted to Canning Purposes; Hints on Cultivation; Prices paid by Packers.

In the South Atlantic and Gulf States the vegetable business has steadily grown, until now the shipments of green vegetables amount to 150,000 carloads per annum. These figures do not include shipments made by water from such ports as Norfolk, Charleston and Savannah, which annually equal 60,000 carloads. The bulk of these shipments are made to the great Eastern and Western markets. The farmers who grow the product realize handsome profits usually, as these shipments are ahead of the local crops, but frequently a decline in the market throws the bulk of the crop back on their hands and makes them heavy losers. To say the least, this is a very precarious business for those who have thus invested their capital.

71

The Eastern and Western States are extensively engaged in raising this class of products which furnish food for the masses in neighboring cities after the Southern trade is over. It requires thousands of farms managed by practical men and millions of dollars.

The growing of vegetables in these sections is necessarily large on account of the immense quantity of raw material used by canning factories. Many grow for this purpose altogether, while others prefer to ship the bulk of their crops to market and dispose of the surplus to the factories.

As the canning industry is not carried on to any great extent in the South many thousand dollars worth of green stock goes to waste. While the South furnishes the North and West with her green product, the North and West furnish the South with the product in hermetically sealed packages. Further, the North and West furnish a good part of the world with this canned product, and both civilized and uncivilized may enjoy the privilege of eating vegetables in and out of season.

In 1889 the exports of canned vegetables amounted to $310,252.00; imports, $389,842.00.

Thus the growing of vegetables in this country is an important item in the food supply of the world, and all varieties of this health-giving food can be found at all seasons of the year.

In growing vegetables for canning purposes great care should be exercised in the selection of seeds, and cheap commission seeds should be especially avoided. The market is flooded with hundreds of varieties of so-called prolific seeds, and for this reason we recommend only

those which our experience has shown to be best suited
to the purpose.

ASPARAGUS.

We give only one variety, Oyster Bay, largely cultivated around New York, as this is a standard variety so
well known and so well adapted to canning. There are
other good varieties but it is very doubtful that they are
equal to this.

Asparagus is propagated by seeds sown in the spring.
The soil should first be well prepared, thoroughly pul-
verized and enriched by well-rotted manure. The seeds
are then sown in rows one foot apart, and should be kept
free of weeds by careful and constant hoeing. The plants
are set out the following spring if they have been properly cultivated, otherwise they will not be large enough
till the second spring after the seeds are sown. One
pound of seeds will produce about 3,000 plants, and
18,000 plants, closely planted, are required to the acre.

For setting out, a bed is previously prepared and the
plants may be set out any time during the spring. The
best mode of planting is in rows three feet apart, the
plants nine inches apart in the rows. Care should be
taken in planting; the roots should be spread out and the
crown covered about three inches. The bed should be
carefully raked over and all germinating weeds destroyed,
in order to give the plants a good start.

Asparagus is best grown in a saline atmosphere, and
for inland districts we would recommend the use of salt
as a spring dressing at the rate of about three pounds to
the square yard. Super-phosphate of lime is also a good

spring dressing, hoeing it in carefully. It takes about three years, sometimes longer, after the seeds are sown before the crop can be marketed. The shoots are cut till about the first of June, when they should be left to grow.

The farmers get good prices in the market for the first of the crop, but not until later in the season, when prices are lower, do they sell to packers, who pay $80 per thousand bunches.

Asparagus is largely packed around New York and requires knowledge and care to put up a good article. The can has an opening on the side instead of on the top, and, after the asparagus is carefully laid in, is filled with water, in which just enough salt has been dissolved to give it a salty taste. This brine may be cold or hot, observing the rule of *exhaust or no exhaust* as in the case of fruits. Packed in 3-lb. tins at a cost of about $3.50 per case. Good demand and margin for select stock.

BEANS, STRING.

Early Valentine, Early Mohawk, Black Wax.

Remarks.—The ground should be well prepared by thorough plowing, and enriched by stable manure and a little super-phosphate of lime. The beans are dropped about three inches apart in drills three inches deep and two feet apart, then covered and the earth pressed upon them with the foot—they will germinate much quicker if covered this way than they will if the earth is merely drawn over them. Plant as early as possible in spring. The yield depends upon season and cultivation, but 150 bushels per acre may be considered the average on fairly good land.

Beans are largely shipped to market in their green state; but when they become plentiful and the price comes down, packers buy liberally, paying about 30 cents per bushel for good stock.

In preparing string beans for the can, all the tough beans should be excluded; then string, break in two the large, place in the blancher and dip in scalding tank where they are allowed three minutes to blanch; then pack in cans and fill with brine as in case of asparagus. Packed in 2-lb. cans at a cost of about $1.00 per case. Fair demand; margin small.

BEANS, LIMA.

Large White Lima, Small White Lima, Seba.

Remarks.—These are the best varieties for canning, the latter being especially esteemed for " succotash." Prepare the ground carefully; make hills, liberally supplied with well rotted stable manure, about 3½ feet apart; in these hills plant 5 or 6 beans, about 2 inches deep. When the plants are out of danger of worms, say about a week old, thin to 2 or 3 in a hill and provide with poles for support of vines. This is a very tender plant, and the seed should not be planted till all danger of frost is over.

The average yield is about 60 bushels of shelled beans to the acre.

Packers pay from 75 cents to $1.00 per bushel, in the pod.

After hulling, which is usually done by hand, these beans are put in the cans which are then filled with brine as in the case of asparagus.

Packed in 2-℔. cans at a cost of about $1.30 per case. Good demand; fair margin.

CORN.

Stowell's Evergreen, Early Egyptian.

Remarks.—The former is the favorite with packers because it remains in the green state longer than any other sort.

The soil best suited to corn, particularly the early, is a sandy loam, thoroughly broken up and well enriched. For good, healthy growth, corn needs warmth, and it should not be planted before warm weather is pretty well assured.   Plant about 9 inches apart in rows $4\frac{1}{2}$ feet apart, and thin out if it comes up too thick.   Some prefer to plant $3\frac{1}{2}$ or 4 feet each way.   The large packer should plant his crop in sections of a week or ten days apart, otherwise some will harden before he can pack it.

Probably more advance has been made in the methods and machinery used in packing corn than in any other, and the packer can turn out ten times the product now that he could twenty years ago.   This branch of the canning industry is now the largest, tomatoes coming next.

Good land will produce about 4 tons per acre.

Packers pay from $5.00 to $6.00 per ton of 2,000 lbs., delivered.

In packing corn, unless in very small lots, we advise the use of corn-cutting machine and corn-silking machine (see special machinery). There is so much competition that the margin of profit is small, and only those who use improved labor-saving machinery can successfully compete in the market. The corn—which must be young and tender, but full grown—is cut from the cob, silked and packed in the cans which are then filled with brine, and it is better to add a little sugar to the brine. Packed in 2-℔. cans at a cost of about $1.20 per case. Canned corn is of a very great commercial importance but the margin is small.

OKRA.

Dwarf, Long Green, Prolific.

Remarks.—This vegetable is most extensively grown in Louisianna and Mississippi, but flourishes throughout the South.

It grows best in damp, rich bottom land; is easy of cultivation, and does not need much attention after the plants get a good start.

Sow in drills 2 inches deep, and from 18 to 24 inches apart in the rows.

Good land, under favorable circumstances, will produce 2 tons to the acre.

It is very nutritious, and is used in soup; also, is packed with tomatoes, as a combination.

Packers pay 75 cents per hundred-weight delivered.

The canned product is just coming into use.

In preparing for the can first throw out all tough, old okra, then remove stems and blanch for 10 minutes in Pea-blanching vessel, described under special machinery;

then pack in the cans which are then filled with brine as described for asparagus.

Packed in 2-℔. cans, at a cost of about $1.60 per case. Fair demand, and pays to pack.

OKRA AND TOMATOES.

This is a very agreeable combination, and is used principally for soup. The okra is blanched for 10 minutes and chopped up, and then combined with an equal quantity of tomatoes.

Packed in 2-℔. and 3-℔. cans, at a cost of about $1.00 and $1.35 per case. Good demand and margin.

PEAS.

Daniel O'Rourke, Extra Early, Champion of England or Marrowfat.

Remarks.—The first and second are what are known as "Early Junes," and are used for the first pack; the other is used for the late pack.

Peas are grown largely for market in their green state, and are shipped to all parts of the country; but in the principal pea-packing districts are cultivated for canning alone. Indeed, there is so much demand for good canned peas that packers sometimes offer such good prices for the green article that it becomes scarce in the market and prices rise.

For growing peas the soil should be well broken up and liberally supplied with well-rotted manure or bone-dust. The peas are sown in drills from 2 to 2½ feet apart. Both varieties call for the same management, except that the Marrowfats require "sticking," while the others do not. As in the case of corn, the crop should be planted in sections a week or so apart. Marrowfats should be planted a little earlier than the others, as they take longer to mature.

The yield of marrowfats is about 100 bushels to the acre, in the pod; that of Early Junes, 75.

Packers pay from $1 to $1.25 per bushel for the first pack; 50 cents to 75 cents for the second pack. Prices depend largely upon the quality and yield.

No article that goes into the can requires greater care in preparation than peas, or pays better for it.

They are first graded with the Pea Separator; then spread on tables and all black eyes and yellow peas removed, by carefully picking them over; then blanched in Pea Blancher till the skin begins to contract, and packed in the can, leaving a space of about $\frac{1}{2}$ inch at top of the can to allow for the swelling of the peas. The cans are then filled with brine—as described for corn.

We maintain that the American pea, carefully graded and packed when young and tender, compares very favorably with the French pea, if indeed it is not fully equal to it, and will in time supplant it. Americans are easily fascinated by foreign names and the fine French peas, like the celebrated French wines, that are served up by the shrewd restaurateur are often nothing more than the genuine American article under a French name.

Peas are packed in 2-℔. cans, at a cost of about $1.50 per case.

There is always a large demand for good peas, and these pay well.

PUMPKIN.

We do not recommend any particular variety to the packer. All farmers have their choice, and any good cooking variety will answer. The cultivation is easy, and immense quantities are raised to the acre. Many farmers plant in hills with corn, omitting every two hills each way, after the corn is up and late enough for the vines not to interfere with the cultivator.

Packers pay about $5 per ton delivered.

In preparing the pumpkin for the can it is first blanched, which is done by putting it in a basket or crate, and lowering into scalding tank for 5 minutes—this process allows the easy removal of the rind, which is done with peeling knives. After peeling it is first sliced, and then grated or mashed; the cans are then packed full, no liquor being used. Pumpkin is extensively canned for making pies, and pays fairly well.

Packed in 3-℔. cans, at a cost of about $1 per case.

SQUASH.

Boston Marrow, Hubbard.

Remarks.—The packing of this vegetable is carried on only to a limited extent, but we recommend the above, —the Boston Marrow an early variety, the Hubbard a late—giving preference to the former.

Plant the Boston Marrow in hills, with a little manure, 4 feet apart; the Hubbard in hills 8 feet apart.

Average yield, 5 tons per acre.

Packers pay $10.00 to $12.00 per ton delivered at factory.

Squash is prepared for the can in about the same manner as pumpkin. The tender varieties need no blanching and are usually mashed in a tub or mortar. Cans to be full, and no liquor used. Fair demand and profit. Packed in 3-lb. cans at a cost of about $1.10 per case.

SUCCOTASH.

This is a very popular combination of corn and beans, ⅔ of the former and ⅓ of the latter. The corn and beans should be young and tender and put up in brine as described for corn. Good demand, and pays to pack. Put up in 2-lb. cans at a cost of about $1.20 per case.

SWEET POTATOES.

Jersey Yam or Yellow Skinned.

Remarks.—We consider the above variety by far the best, though others are used.

The sweet potato flourishes best in a light, warm soil enriched by manure, and matures perfectly in Southern latitudes. The tubers are set in a draw bed in early Spring, and when the plants are several inches high they are transplanted to ridges 3 feet apart, the plants about 1 foot apart in the ridges. The ground should be pretty well enriched. They are worked by throwing the earth up to them from the middle of the row with a plow. Tubers mature in 4 months. The canned potatoe is extensively used for pies.

The first process in packing sweet potatoes is to blanch them, which is done by putting them in the process crate,

6

having first put wire netting on the bottom and around the sides, and then lowering the crate in the process tank and letting it remain there until the skin of the potatoes begins to crack or they are about three-fourths cooked. They are then taken on forks, the skin removed as quickly as possible, sliced, quartered and immediately packed in the cans without liquor. In exhausting do not lower the crate deep enough to admit water into the cans as they are dry packed. Packed in 3-lb. cans at a cost of about $1.10 per case.

The average yield is 8 tons to the acre. Packers pay $15.00 to $20.00 per ton delivered at factory.

TOMATOES.

Acme, Trophy, Champion, New Queen.

Remarks.—The Trophy is probably the favorite. The tomato is the most important of all the vegetables for canning, and is extensively grown for this purpose alone.

The seeds are sown in hot-beds in early Spring, and when all danger of frost is past the plants are transferred to hills about 3 feet apart, each way, and containing a spadeful of well rotted manure. A light sandy loam is best.

Probably no vegetable varies more in yield than the tomatoe, but a fair average yield is 400 bushels to the acre.

Packers pay about 20 cents per bushel or $7.00 per ton generally, though as high as 45 cents per bushel is sometimes paid. The price depends upon the yield and quality.

Tomatoes, like corn and peaches, are recognized as staple articles of food and always in season. Nearly every cannery in the country packs this vegetable, and in

Maryland, outside of Baltimore, it is packed almost exclusively. In packing, the tomatoes are first scalded by placing them in a wire basket, or better still a Tomato Scalder, and dipping into a scalding tank just long enough to loosen the skin. They are then peeled, 3 cents a bucket being paid for this, passed to the packing table, packed as solid as possible in the cans which are then placed on the capping tray and passed to the capper who solders on the cap, leaving open the exhaust or vent. Tomatoes are put up in 2-℔. and 3-℔. cans at a cost of about 90 cts. per case of former, $1.20 per case of latter. Good demand and margin.

TO PACKERS.

NOTE.—It is impossible to state exactly what prices are paid by the packers of the country for their raw material, as prices paid are governed entirely by the season, quality, and section of country. Hence, in making contracts one must use his own judgment. We have, however, given a scale of prices which will guide the packer. The condition of the product offered should be carefully looked into, and the price graded accordingly. If a packer rushes ahead and commences an early pack he will have to pay higher prices than he will if he waits a while till the raw material becomes more plentiful. On the other hand if he waits too long he will not be able to make a full pack before the season is over, besides he will run the risk of getting inferior material. These considerations, together with the prospective prices of the canned product, should guide him in his course of action. Great care and judgment is needed in this business and one cannot afford to go into it until he has carefully considered the situation. He should examine the crop reports, see where he can place his goods and at what probable price. He should have a thorough knowledge of the situation both as regards present prices and the outlook of raw material and canned goods. It often happens that in some sections there is a full yield of fruits or vegetables while in others not more than half a yield.

(2)

PROCESSES.

Open-bath and Closed-top Steam Kettles.

The above kettles being adapted to both fruits and vegetables alike, the remarks under "Processes" for fruit will apply here. However, the following vegetables: asparagus, corn, lima beans, peas, string beans, okra and succotash, require closed-top steam kettles, unless chloride of calcium is used in which case the required degree of heat can be obtained with open-bath kettles. But we do not advise the use of calcium, and where the above vegetables are packed closed-top process should be employed in all cases.

ASPARAGUS.

"Standard:" Cans to be full, asparagus to be young and tender, liquor clear.

Exhaust cans 10 minutes at 212°.

Closed-top: allow 30 minutes process at 240°.

BEANS, STRING.

"Standard:" Cans full, beans young and tender, carefully strung, packed during growing season, liquor clear.

Exhaust cans 10 minutes at 212°.

Closed-top: allow 40 minutes process at 240°.

BEANS, LIMA.

"Standard:" Cans full of green beans, liquor clear.
Exhaust cans 10 minutes at 212°.
Closed-top: allow 35 minutes process at 240°.

CORN.

"Standard:" Sweet corn only to be used, cut from the
cob while young and tender, cans to cut out full of
corn, liquor clear.
Exhaust cans 10 minutes at 212°.
Closed-top: allow 40 minutes process at 240°.

OKRA.

"Standard:" Cans to be full, okra to be young and ten-
der, liquor clear.
Exhaust cans 10 minutes at 212°.
Closed-top: allow 25 minutes process at 240°.

OKRA AND TOMATOES.

"Standard:" Okra to be young and tender, and cut up.
Tomatoes to be of good ripe fruit.
Exhaust cans 10 minutes at 212°.
Open-bath: allow 35 minutes process at 212°.
Closed top: allow 15 minutes process at 240°.

PEAS.

"Standard:" Cans to be full of young and tender peas,
free from yellow or black eyes, clear liquor.

Exhaust cans 10 minutes at 212°.

Closed-top: allow 20 minutes process at 240° on Early Junes.

Closed-top: allow 25 minutes process at 240° on Marrowfats.

PUMPKIN.

"Standard:" Cans to be as solid packed as possible, free from lumps and of good color.

Exhaust cans 10 minutes at 212°.

Open-bath: allow 40 minutes process at 212°.

Closed-top: allow 15 minutes process at 240°.

SQUASH.

"Standard:" Cans to be full, squash young and tender, chopped and mashed.

Exhaust cans 10 minutes at 212°.

Open-bath: allow 40 minutes process at 212°.

Closed-top: allow 15 minutes process at 240°.

SUCCOTASH.

"Standard:" Cans to be full of green corn and beans, $\frac{2}{3}$ of former and $\frac{1}{3}$ of latter, clear liquor.

Exhaust cans 10 minutes at 212°.

Closed-top: allow 40 minutes process at 240°.

SWEET POTATOES.

"Standard:" Cans to be full, dry packed, cooked in exhaust kettle till three-fourths done, then peeled, halved and quartered.

Exhaust cans 5 minutes at 212°.

Open-bath : allow 15 minutes process at 212°.

Closed-top : allow 5 minutes process at 240°.

TOMATOES.

"Standard :" Cans to be reasonably solid, of good ripe
fruit, cold packed.

Exhaust cans 10 minutes at 212°.

Open-bath : allow 30 minutes process at 212° for 3-℔.

Open-bath : allow 22 minutes process at 212° for 2-℔.

Closed-top : allow 10 minutes process at 240° for 3-℔.

Closed-top : allow 8 minutes process at 240° for 2-℔.

V.

FISH.

General Remarks; Varieties best adapted to Canning Purposes; Fish Culture; Prices paid by Packers, and Location of Fishing Grounds.

Some idea may be formed of the enormous magnitude of the fish industry when statistics show that in 1881 nearly 200,000 tons of fish came into the London market, and that this supply is rapidly increasing. Most of these were taken in the North Sea which is probably the most productive fishing grounds in the world. Then come the herring and cod fisheries off the coast of Labrador and New England, the sardine fisheries off the coast of Brittany, the lobster fisheries of Maine and Canada, the oyster beds of the Chesapeake, the salmon fisheries of the Pacific coast.* All the various branches of this great industry employ thousands of vessels, tens of thousands of men and millions of money, and furnish food to the population of almost the entire globe. There

88

are very few people whose diet does not consist largely
of fish. Any one who has visited the Fulton Fish
Market in New York has some conception of what an
important factor is fish in the food supply of our great
cities. When we reflect that the waters from pole to pole
are teeming with countless billions of fish, fed and reared
on the bounties of the deep and only waiting to be
caught and brought to the consumer, we may with reason praise the generosity of Old Ocean. No other part
of the globe offers such a bountiful supply of cheap,
wholesome food to the millions of inhabitants.

As far as the fear of deep-sea fish, such as herring and
cod, being killed out, is concerned, we believe there is
little reason for it. From time immemorial it has been
a custom to circulate periodic gloomy reports of the
rapid decimation of certain fish, coupled with prophecies
that in a few years they would be extinct. These prophecies have never proved true; but, on the contrary, the
supply has almost always continued to increase, which
may have been partly due to improved methods of
catching. The number of fish taken from the seas by
man must be insignificant as compared with that which
is killed in other ways; for, a female herring, for instance, lays 25,000 eggs and at this rate the millions of
herrings in the sea would soon multiply to such an
extent that the waters could not hold them. Further,
the female cod yields about 5,000,000! At this rate how
long would the ocean give sufficient breathing and feeding room for its fish? The case is different with the help-
less oyster, which is completely at the mercy of men who
know no mercy; the salmon and other fish whose breed-

ing and feeding grounds are limited to certain localities
of small area and usually in shallow water. Of these we
shall speak later. Referring the reader for detailed information on the many varieties of fish, their localities, hab-
its, culture, etc., to any of the many books on the subject,
we will take up in order the few kinds that are canned.

CLAMS.

There are two kinds of clams commonly used for food
in this country: the large clam and the little neck clam.
The former is chopped up and stewed or made into
chowder; the latter is either baked or eaten raw. This
shell fish, though plentiful along the coasts of England,
Norway and other parts of Europe is not used there for
food, and may be considered as distinctly an American
dish. It is found in large numbers buried in the mud
along the shores of our salt waters. It is canned either
in the form of chowder or after the manner of oysters as
given below, except that it requires a longer process.
The process given will answer for either form.

Packed in 1-℔., 2-℔. and 3-℔. cans.

NOTE.—We advise the use of closed-top steam kettles for processing all kinds of fish.

CRABS.

The common salt water crab abounds in all of our salt
waters and is too well known to need description. It is
usually caught in comparatively shallow water, not far
from shore, by means of a seine, or a dip-net and a line
baited with fresh fish or fresh meat, though the salt article
is sometimes used but with less success. The crab which

resembles the lobster in so many respects differs from it very distinctly in its choice of food, for while the former detests tainted meat or fish the latter prefers it to the fresh sound article. The canning of crabs is a comparatively new thing, and the business is quite extensively carried on in some of the towns along the Eastern Shore of the Chesapeake Bay.

In preparing crabs for the can they are first boiled in a large caldron till about three-fourths cooked. The meat is then removed from the shells, cracker crumbs added to it, and it is then packed solid, without liquor, in the cans which are then wiped, capped and exhausted, tipped and processed.

Packed in 1-℔. and 2-℔. cans; 4 dozen of the former and 2 dozen of the latter are put in a case. Empty shells at the rate of 4 for each pound of crab, accompany each case, and when the cans are opened the crab is put into these shells, seasoned and baked in the usual way.

LOBSTERS.

The lobster ranks with the oyster in point of importance as a food-fish, either in the fresh state or in the canned form, and they are both alike threatened with destruction by greedy fishermen on the one side and negligent legislation on the other. There are about 2,500,000 cans of lobster annually eaten in the United States and of these not more than 15 or 20 per cent are put up in Maine, where alone they are packed in the Union, the rest are imported mostly from Canada. Twenty-five years ago lobsters, of what we now consider

an enormous size, were plentiful from New Jersey to
Rhode Island but they are now practically extinct along
these shores and are found in significant numbers only in
Maine. Even there they will be exterminated unless better and enforced laws are enacted for their protection.
We are glad to see that some of the New Englanders
are beginning to open their eyes and to devise measures
for checking the indiscriminate slaughter of this excellent shell-fish and protecting the few that remain. By
all means have a good long close season and let it be
strictly enforced. We can doubtless take profitable les-
sons from the Provinces on this subject. We are glad
to learn that our countrymen on the Pacific coast are
taking active steps toward propagating the lobster there.
We see no reason why it should not thrive there and we
wish the promoters of this enterprise every success. Why
not re-stock the Rhode Island and New Jersey waters,
and protect by stringent laws? Experience has shown
that these waters are particularly well suited to the purpose.

The British Isles, once so bountifully supplied with
lobsters by her own waters, are now largely dependent
for their supply upon Norway which comes next to the
Canadian Provinces in the importance of her lobster
fisheries.

The value of the lobster as a nutritive food is main-
tained by the best medical authorities.

For canning they are three-fourths cooked in the same
manner as crabs; the meat is then carefully removed
from the shells and packed solid in the cans, which are
then filled with brine containing 3 per cent. salt, wiped,

capped, exhausted, tipped and processed. Packed in 1-℔. cans, 4 doz. to a case, and 2-℔. cans, 2 doz. to a case.

OYSTERS.

In 1800 a million oysters were taken off the British coasts, and the catch increased till the high figure of 72,000,000 was reached in a single season, since which time the catch has decreased until now but few oysters are caught there.

The same scarcity is, or has been till lately, true of almost every European country on the coast of which the oyster is found. What is the cause of this state of affairs? Over dredging has undoubtedly been one prime cause, yet those who believe that a "close time" would rectify this matter are confronted by the best authorities who say that it is ridiculous to protect the oyster fisheries during 4 months of the year and allow the dredgers to denude them during the remaining eight.

The fact is there are other forces at work in nature itself rendering the rapid multiplication of this bivalve a somewhat doubtful problem. The oyster has an extremely delicate constitution; extremes of either heat or cold are fatal to it and particularly so to its "spat." It is supposed that out of one or two millions of progeny produced by the oyster not more than a half-dozen ever reach maturity. It is not known just how long the "larva" oyster remains in its free and active condition, but there is very great reason to believe that it is at least several days, so that detached from the parent it might be carried 70 or 80 miles from the place of its birth before passing into its next condition. The young oyster grows to about 3 inches across by the end of its third year and is then considered very edible, but it is better to leave it a year longer. It will live for about 20 years. An important point is the condition of existence in its natural state. In the first place, it is dependent upon a certain degree of salinity of water, and it is doubted that they breed or do well unless the water contains 3 per cent. or more of salt. In the second place, it is extremely sensitive to heat and cold and in shallow water large numbers perish from these two causes.

Oysters are still taken in small quantities along the English coasts, but France has made the most progress in their culture and has been amply repaid for, instead of the gloomy outlook of a few years since, the industry is prosperous and promising. France with her present laws and systematic cultivation need not fear the extinction of this wholesome fish.

The Seaboard of Virginia, North Carolina, South Carolina and Georgia were once famed for their supplies, —Virginia alone having an area of 2,000,000 acres covered with them. Long Island, with her 115 miles of oyster coast and numerous smaller beds, is slowly but surely being denuded of her supply.

With reference to the exhaustion of oyster beds Prof. G. Brown Goode says that in the case of fixed animals, like the sponge, the mussel, the clam and the oyster, the colonies or beds may be exterminated exactly as a forest may be cut down. He mentions the oyster beds of Pocomoke Sound, Maryland, which have been choked and virtually destroyed by the rubbish raked over them, and the destruction of the ledges suitable for the reception of the young spat by careless dredgers. He further says that the preservation of the oyster beds is a matter of vital importance to the United States, for oyster fishing unsupported by oyster culture will soon deprive thousands of men of employment and millions of people of a cheap and favorite food. He adds that the present unregulated methods will probably prevail till the dredging of the natural beds ceases to be remunerative, when the oyster industry will be transferred from the improvident fisherman to the care-taking oyster culturist.

Already steps are being taken looking to the cultivation of the oyster in New York waters. "The bottom of Long Island Sound is being laid off into townships, sections, quarter sections and lots, and the land sold by auction. The scheme is not a real estate speculation however. It is a bona fide sale of perpetual franchises of submerged lands, suitable to the cultivation of oysters. The survey and sale of lands is conducted by the Fish Commissioners of the State of New York, under authority vested in them by an act of the legislature passed last year. This law applies to all of the lands under the waters of the State suitable for shell-fish culture, but is of the most importance in reference to the lands under Long Island Sound, Staten Island Sound and Princess Bay. Most of the lands are in the neighborhood of the old natural growth oyster beds. These beds are free to all, but as they contain only an inferior quality and are not extensive enough to supply the demand, artificial beds are necessary. Twenty-five years ago, the oyster supply came almost entirely from the natural beds. Owing to reckless and excessive tonging and dredging of the beds, and to the pollution of the waters by the establishment of oil refineries and factories in their vicinity, these beds have deteriorated and in many cases entirely disappeared. The importance of the industry is shown by the fact that upward of 7,000 men are engaged in the business in New York State, and that a capital of over $6,000,000 is represented. The condition of the industry before the matter was taken in hand by the commissioners was getting to be hopelessly involved. Under the new system the State Fish Commissioners are authorized to survey all lands suitable for shell-fish culture and to sell perpetual franchises for plots not exceeding 500 acres in extent to any one applicant. A charge of $1 per acre is made for unoccupied lands; and if there is more than one applicant the plot is put up at auction and sold to the highest bidder. If the land is already occupied and cultivated in good faith the plot is sold to the occupant at the nominal rate of 10c per acre to pay for the cost of surveying and mapping. The land under water is laid out in townships 1,000 acres, quarter section of 250 acres, and 100 acre lots." If Maryland had such a provision for the cultivation and protection of the oyster what might we not expect of the Chesapeake Bay with its 6,000 square miles of suitable area? But with the present foolish laws it is a matter of a few years at most when the oyster industry of the Chesapeake Bay will be a thing of the past. This industry, as at present conducted, instead of being a blessing to the state is a positive loss, as the Governor in his last message stated that the State oyster navy entailed

from $2,000 to $3,000 expenses over and above what
was derived from licenses. Whereas, if it were properly
conducted it would give employment to the oysterman
the entire year instead of only a few months as it does now.
Both the shipping of raw oysters and the canning industry, which is already moving away from us on account
of scarcity and high prices, are jeopardized. Prices
have advanced while the oysters have deteriorated both
in size and quality, for they are caught so fast that they
cannot mature. If oyster grounds were leased in Maryland the State would derive a great pecuniary advantage
and at the same time arrest the wholesale destruction of
the beds.

The writer has made a careful survey of the oyster
grounds of the South and finds the industry rapidly
developing but greatly in need of proper legislation,
although the States are beginning to see the need and
importance of such legislation and to give it their consideration. Virginia and North Carolina are rigidly en-
forcing their Oyster Laws, and Georgia has taken steps
toward protecting her beds and those who cultivate them.
Still there are certain restrictions yet to be placed. Dr.
Oemler of Wilmington Island, Ga., who cultivates the
oyster to quite an extent, wisely conceived the importance
of the industry, and the present law is due to him in a very
great measure. South Carolina has also taken measures
for furthering the interests of her oyster industry. The
fact is, this great industry is moving South as is attested
by the thousands of barrels of oysters received from that
section in the New York, Eastern and Western markets.
The canning branch of the business is also drifting to the

coasts of the South Atlantic and Gulf States, and many large factories are located along the coasts of North Carolina, Florida, Alabama and Mississippi. It has been said by Northern oystermen that the Southern oyster could not compare with the New York or Chesapeake oyster, but we have eaten both and can truthfully say that we have found oysters in some sections of the South fully equal to the Northern article. In some sections of the South, however, they are not so good : for example, at Pensacola, Fla., though plentiful, they do not open up well, are rather salt, without flavor, and have a dark look and black gills.

For the benefit of those of our canners who are seeking openings South, we give below a few hints as to the location of her beds. It would be well to look carefully into the laws of each State before making final locations. Due consideration is here allowed for convenient transportation as this is a most important item to be considered by both packers and shippers of oysters. Norfolk, Va., though having a large oyster industry, is so well known and so conveniently situated with reference to the Eastern and Northern markets that the raw material commands a good price, and we think therefore that those looking for factory locations will find further South places that are better suited for purchasing raw stock. For instance : Elizabeth City, Washington, New Berne, Morehead City, Federal Point at the mouth of Cape Fear River, all of which are in North Carolina and afford excellent shipping facilities. For South Carolina we would recommend a location at Georgetown which affords good facilities both for securing raw stock and for shipping; also Winyah Bay, which is a natural oyster ground and conveniently located; Port Royal would be an excellent location, with good facilities, were it not for the scarcity of labor which finds employment in the great phosphate and fertilizer works located here and at Beaufort. For Georgia, we would recommend a location at Savannah, or better still, Tybee Island which has good shipping facilities and would save the trip up Savannah River. We found better oysters here than at any of the other places we visited; it seems to be the natural feeding grounds. We never tasted better bivalves than those taken from Daufuskie, or Calabouge Sound; the latter beds seemed to have been untouched, judging from the quantities our tongs brought up. This Sound is well adapted to dredging. It is near Tybee that oysters are being cultivated; a stock company, with ample capital, has been formed, under the laws of Georgia. Daufuskie and Calabouge Sound are in South Carolina, just at the mouth of the Savannah River, and concessions may be had from the State for the privilege of fishing there.

Other places around Savannah offer excellent locations except that the shipping facilities are not so good. The leading shipping points are Thunderbolt, Isle of Hope, and Cedar Hammock; the latter has oysters of fine quality but in limited quantities. For other locations in Georgia we would recommend St. Simon's and Brunswick, for these places have fine shipping facilities, and a territory so large that the supply is practically inexhaustible if the proper methods of protection are used. Here we also find a company engaged in the cultivation of the oyster, the Brunswick Oyster Cultivation and Packing Co.

For Florida : Fernandina is a good location, for the oysters are plentiful, the territory large, and the shipping facilities particularly good; then comes Daytona, or New Smyrna at the mouth of Mosquito Inlet, where we find the same conditions existing as in the Chesapeake Bay, being especially adapted to the growing of the oyster. There is a good supply at the inlet of the Indian River but they are not so good, being very like those of Pensacola. Still further South along the coast to Miami we find a plentiful supply, but lack of good transportation facilities puts them out of reach of the markets of the country. In time, however, this will be a great place for this industry for there is a plentiful supply of the raw stock and everything is suited for growing. At Key West a few oysters are taken but the business does not amount to much. Along the Gulf coast they are very abundant and are taken in large quantities, but new and apparently inexhaustible beds are constantly being discovered. This section would be a veritable gold mine if it were not so remote from the great markets. . From Key West to Punta Rassa there is every evidence of great quantities of oysters; from Punta Rassa to Cedar Keys the industry is carried on to a greater extent; and we had the pleasure of eating some very fine specimens of this succulent bivalve along the coast adjacent to the Manatee, Crystal and Swaunnee Rivers. Transportation lines are opening up this country, but at present Cedar Keys is the shipping point. From Cedar Keys to Mobile Bay oysters are found in. the greatest abundance, and we recommend the following places for locations; St. Mark's, Appalachicola, and a place near Mobile,— the latter place having superior shipping facilities and is giving due consideration to this growing industry and already an immense business is being done here. The above localities are possessed of natural grounds for the growing of the oyster, but let those interested take warning from the example of the Northern oyster beds, and not carry their catching to such an extent as to exhaust this great wealth. California realizes the importance of this great industry, but here the oyster does not seem to thrive, and an immense quantity of the canned product finds its way to her coast. Millions of seed oysters have been transplanted there from the East, but with little success. Here we would call the attention of Maryland legislators to the manner in which they allow the Chesapeake beds to be destroyed by the hundreds of vessels engaged in the traffic of transplanting seed oysters to the Delaware and Long Island beds. How can our legislators expect oysters to multiply, or even to remain at what they are, in our waters, under such conditions? But possibly they do not think anything about it. Maryland affords a most excellent illustration of what foolish legislation, or perhaps we might say no legislation at all, can do toward crushing the life out of an important industry. Year after year the innocent oyster makes its appearance before the august assembly of *Solons* and pleads for a little longer lease on its native haunts, but is sent away without any definite answer. The subject is most prolific in discussion and suggestions and most barren in conclusions. Some hint that it is not to the interest of some of our legislators to settle the oyster question, and that this periodic wrangling over the toothsome bivalves is analogous to the wrangling of a lot of lawyers over a case whose fat fees cease as soon as it is settled. If they are not careful the goose that lays the golden egg will die through neglect,—it would be policy to administer to its necessities at least to the extent of keeping it alive.

For oyster canning, the factory should be located as near as possible to the oyster grounds and where ample transportation facilities are to be had. It should also be as near as possible to the water which should be of sufficient depth for boats to come up and unload at all tides, and a wharf is almost indispensable. Steaming boxes are necessary. The oysters are unloaded from the "sloop" immediately into oyster cars made of strap-iron, 2½ feet wide by 6 feet long, and deep enough to hold about 5 bushels. These cars are mounted on wheels and run on tracks leading from the steaming box out to the edge of the wharf, so that the oyster can be run directly into the steaming box which is air-tight. The steam is then turned on, and in a few minutes the oysters open their shells, the cars are then run out on side tracks to the shuckers who immediately shuck them at 20 cents per gallon.

After the oysters have been shucked the liquor is drained off and they are rinsed in cold water and filled into the cans in the following quantities:

No. 1 cans, 6 oz., Standard.
No. 2 cans, 12 oz., Standard.
No. 1 cans, 5 oz., Standard.

No. 2 cans, 10 oz., Standard.

No. 1 cans, 4 oz.

No. 2 cans, 8 oz;

No. 1 cans, 1½ oz., Light weights.

No. 2 cans, 3 oz., Light weights.

A very good way for steaming oysters is to have the cars built close, or long boxes may be constructed as tight as possible; then have a pipe leading from the boiler to the place where the oysters are unloaded and here connect it with the cars or boxes, turn on steam—and your oysters are ready for the shuckers in a few minutes. This method saves the expense of the usual steaming box, which is considerable.

After the cans have received their proper weights of oysters they are filled with a brine containing 3 per cent. of salt. (*It is a well known fact that oysters will not keep in their own liquor.*) The cans are then wiped, capped, exhausted, tipped and processed.

Packers pay for common steam "Cove" oysters 50 cents to 55 cents per bushel; for best steam stock, 60 cents to 65 cents per bushel. One bushel of the former will turn out about 45 ounces of meat; the latter, about 52 ounces.

SALMON.

The canning of salmon is the most important of the fish-canning industries, and is at present confined almost exclusively to Southeastern Alaska. But few persons outside of those engaged in it have any conception of its vastness. It would be idle guesswork for us to attempt to say whether these fish are inexhaustible but it is certain that up to this time it looks as though they were. However, we remember when they were in the same immense quantities in the McCloud and Sacramento Rivers of California; but alas, the fishermen there were like the oystermen of the Chesapeake and now, as a result of their war of extermination, but few salmon are taken in these rivers. In the Columbia River, so famous for its salmon, where vast numbers were caught but a few years since, they are getting so scarce that at the present rate of decrease they would soon become extinct. But happily the U. S. Government has begun to appreciate the importance of the industry and to take measures for propagating by establishing hatcheries on the Columbia River and in other sections.

This wise course has been adopted none too soon, for at the present rate of extermination it would be but a few years, at most, when this great fish would be a luxury to be eaten by the rich alone, if indeed it did not disappear altogether from our waters.

Alaska is now the great salmon fishing and canning ground, and it remains to be seen how long this fine fish can survive the ruthless war in that region. Canneries exist here in great numbers and their daily output during the season amounts to millions of cans. One concern alone, recently incorporated in Chicago for operating factories in Alaska, has invested $1,000,000 in the business. The variety canned for commercial purposes is the silver salmon, about 10 cents apiece being paid for them. The fishing is done largely by natives who are furnished with nets for the purpose.

San Francisco is the great salmon market and controls fully two-thirds of the output of the Alaska canning establishments. The product is consumed mostly in this country, but we also export large quantities, principally to England.

We proceed to describe the method of preparing salmon for the can, and the same method applies to the red snapper, sea trout and all similar fish. First remove scales and entrails and cut off the heads, then wash *carefully* in clear warm water, net and lower into process tank till about three-fourths cooked; then, without removing bones, pack solid in cans, which are then filled with a brine containing 3 per cent. salt, wiped, capped, exhausted, tipped and processed. Some fish are put up with mustard, some with tomatoes, some with oil; indeed we may say that fish may be packed any way to suit the taste, the processing being the consideration that concerns the keeping qualities. Size of cans used are mostly 1-lb. and 2-lb., sometimes 3-lb.

SARDINES.

The sardines that are packed in this country are not true sardines but young herrings. These herring-sardine factories are confined to Maine, where there are between 40 and 50, with an annual output of about 90,000,000 boxes. These little fish, though put up in cotton-seed oil instead of olive oil, are evidently liked here for they have almost entirely supplanted the French sardines very few of which are now imported. This is doubtless partly due to the cheapness of the American article as compared with the French. We are inclined to think that the fine

flavor of the latter is due as much to the care taken in
their preparation and the use of pure olive oil as to any
inherent property of the fish itself, which should be carefully cleaned and packed as soon as possible after being
taken from the water.

France undoubtedly furnishes the finest sardines in the
market, and she has long had undisputed control of the
sardine industry.   But the French Government takes a
lively interest in her fishermen and assists them in many
ways.   There are engaged in her sardine industry over
4,000 vessels and 20,000 fishermen.   But her canned
product trade has fallen off somewhat of late, partly
from the substitution of the American article and partly
from the rivalry of Portugal where the genuine sardines
are plentiful and numerous factories have been established.   The silly custom of Maine packers putting
French labels on their boxes has done the American
industry much harm, and the sooner they quit it the
better.

The method of preparing herring-sardines for the can,
or rather box, in this country differs from that employed
by the French and Portuguese for true sardines.   With
us, the young herrings are taken from the large nets in
scoop-nets and thrown *en masse* into boats, then carried
ashore and piled up on long tables.   Their heads are
first cut off, entrails removed, after which they are rinsed
in warm water and then placed on gridirons or "flakes"
over a hot fire and broiled till about half cooked.   This
work is done almost exclusively by small children.   The
fish are taken from the "flakes" and packed in flat rec-
tangular tin boxes, with rounded corners, each box hold-

ing from 8 to 10 fish, according to size. The boxes are then filled with hot cotton-seed oil, or sometimes mustard, wiped, capped and processed. These boxes cost, to pack, from 5 to 8 cents each and are put up in cases of one hundred boxes each.

The foreigners differ from us in the following points : The sardines when taken from the nets are carefully placed in layers in baskets and thus conveyed to the factory. In fine weather they are dried in the sun, at other times, artificially. After drying they are about half cooked in olive oil which is then drained off, and the fish packed in tins which are then filled with hot olive oil, wiped, capped and processed. The French have their sardines packed in the tins within 24 hours from the time they are taken from the water. Sardines being packed while hot, in small tins, need no exhaust.

SNAPPER (RED).

This fish is one of the finest in Southern waters, and is rarely ever taken in Northern latitudes. Fine snapper banks are located off Fernandina, Fla., to a point south to Bay Biscayne on the South Atlantic, but the great banks are situated directly off Cape Canaveral. These fish are also caught on the Gulf coast in large numbers, Pensacola being a shipping point for them, and hundreds are engaged in catching them. The fishing on the Atlantic banks is mostly conducted by Northern fishermen, each vessel taking along about 10 tons of ice for preserving their catches amounting to several thousand fish which are caught in about two days, taken to Savannah and shipped by steamer to the New York market.

The small snapper retails at from 15 cents to 30 cents per ℔., the large ones from 10 cents to 20 cents per ℔. This fish is well adapted to canning, and we think a superior article to the salmon, but the canning factories would have to be located at points near the fishing grounds where the fish can be bought for one cent per ℔. delivered. New Smyrna or Appalachicola, Fla., would be an excellent location. Prepared and packed like salmon, except that the bones are removed.

TROUT (SEA).

The sea trout is taken at various points along the Atlantic coast from Massachusetts south to Key West, Fla., and considerable numbers are caught on the Gulf coast also. The mode of catching is generally with nets. As this fish frequents the shores and goes in large schools they are highly esteemed and make an excellent canning fish for which purpose about 3 cents per ℔. is paid.

Prepared and packed like snapper, except that it is usually spiced, sometimes packed with tomato sauce.

TURTLE.

It is not necessary to say anything in praise of the turtle which is considered such a delicacy and commands such high prices at all seasons. For canning, the Green Turtle is used and is highly prized for making soups. It is taken in Southern latitudes, principally along the Florida coast from the mouth of the Indian River to Key West, Fla. The latter place is largely engaged in the catching and shipping of turtle.

Turtle is canned principally in the form of soup, which

is made as usually served and put while boiling hot in the cans which are then wiped, capped, tipped and processed. If it is desired to can the meat this is done by simply cooking about three-fourths; then packing in the cans, which are then wiped, capped, exhausted, tipped and processed.

NOTE.—Any kind of soup or fish may be prepared to suit the taste, in the form in which they are usually served in the so-called fresh state, then canned; but it is customary to cook them till about three-fourths cooked, before they are put in the can, the rest of the cooking being done by processing.

(2)

PROCESSES.

CLAMS.

Exhaust cans 10 minutes at 212°.
Allow for 1-℔. cans a process of 20 minutes at 240°.
Allow for 2-℔. cans a process of 25 minutes at 240°.

CRABS.

Exhaust cans 5 minutes at 212°.
Allow for 1-℔. cans a process of 10 minutes at 240°.
Allow for 2-℔. cans a process of 12 minutes at 240°.

LOBSTER.

Exhaust cans 10 minutes at 212°.
Allow for 1-℔. cans a process of 15 minutes at 240°.
Allow for 2-℔. cans a process of 20 minutes at 240°.

OYSTERS.

Exhaust cans 10 minutes at 212°.

Allow for No. 1 cans, 6 oz., a process of 16 minutes at 240°.

Allow for No. 2 cans, 12 oz., a process of 20 minutes at 240°.

Allow for No. 1 cans, 5 oz., a process of 14 minutes at 240°.

Allow for No. 2 cans, 10 oz., a process of 18 minutes at 240°.

SALMON, RED SNAPPER AND SEA TROUT.

Exhaust cans 10 minutes at 212°.

Allow for 1-℔. cans a process of 15 minutes at 240°.

Allow for 2-℔. cans a process of 20 minutes at 240°.

SARDINES.

Allow boxes a process of 10 minutes at 240°.

TURTLE AND ALL SOUPS.

Exhaust cans 5 minutes at 212°.

Allow 1-℔. cans a process of 10 minutes at 240°.

Allow 2-℔. cans a process of 12 minutes at 240°.

Allow 3-℔. cans a process of 15 minutes at 240°.

VI.

MEATS.

(1)

General Remarks.

The canning of meats is confined chiefly to beef and mutton, the former being the most extensive. Besides these, poultry and ham are put up; and potted turkey, potted chicken, etc., are gradually growing in favor with the people, the trade in these having been developed mainly within the last few years. In regard to the fresh beef industry of this country it is so enormous that it is almost impossible to give definite figures. It has been estimated that the present population of the United States consume about two billion dollars worth of meats per annum,—a very large portion of this is beef. In Kansas, Nebraska, Texas, New Mexico, Wyoming, Colorado, Montana and other parts of the West, are 1,600,-000 square miles of as fine grazing lands as are to be found in the world, over which roam thousands of herds of cattle and flocks of sheep, numbering from 100 to 20,000 head each. Beef and mutton are the staple meats of this country and, in fact, the civilized world, and the great advantage of the canned article, on account of its keeping qualities and convenience of transportation, is at once apparent.

The exports of canned beef for 1889 amounted to $4,375,000—pretty good figures at first sight, but very low in reality when we consider the quantity and quality of our raw product and the populous countries that are dependent, for their meat supply, on others. We believe there is an unjust discrimination against American canned meat abroad, though a part of the prejudice is doubtless caused by such trickery as was shown in the recent bogus mutton case exposed in London.

There is no reason why we should not, with our factory and transportation facilities, double or treble our exports of canned meats in a short time and we can easily do so by using honesty and push.

Both South America and Australia have immense areas of fine grazing lands and during the last ten years have done wonders in the quality and quantity of cattle and sheep they have raised; the sheep being particularly fine. These countries are already our formidable competitors in European markets and will be more so when they become more fully acquainted with the art of canning. Hence the double necessity of our putting up first class goods and placing them on the market in the right way.

BEEF.

Beef is prepared for the can in more ways, and the canned product is of greater commercial importance, than any other meat. First we have the *smoked and dried beef*, commonly called chipped beef on account of the form in which it is usually served, which is cut into small thin slices and packed solid into the cans, mostly 1-℔. Then we have *corned beef*, which is boiled till thoroughly done, to admit of its easy removal from the bone, boned and packed as solid as possible in the cans. Corned beef is packed in 1-℔. cans, 2 dozen cans to the case; 2-℔., 4-℔. and 6-℔. cans, 1 dozen to the case; and 14-℔. cans, ½ dozen to the case. *Fresh beef* is canned in either the *boiled, roasted* or *potted* form. The former is prepared and packed in the same manner as corned beef, but a little salt should be added to the water in which it is boiled, and it is generally put up in 2-℔. cans, 3 dozen to the case. To can roast beef, the beef may be thoroughly roasted in large pieces, boned, seasoned and packed in the same manner, and same size can as the boiled; but the best grade of this article is obtained by selecting choice cuts, sprinkling well with salt or other seasoning, roasting thoroughly and packing *whole* in flat cans. To put up potted beef, the beef should be roasted, rather than boiled, as it will thus retain more of its natural juices and flavor. After being well cooked it is boned and run through a cutter which cuts it up uniformly fine; it is then highly seasoned with pepper, salt and other condiments to suit the taste, and packed solid in the cans, usually 10-oz. cans, 2 dozen to the case. Beef tongue is canned in either the potted form in the same manner as beef, in 10-oz. cans, 2 dozen to the case, and 5-oz. cans, 4 dozen to the case; or, whole, in 1½-℔., 2-℔. and 2½-℔. cans, 1 dozen to the case.

8

FOWL.

Chicken, duck, turkey and all kinds of fowl, are put up in the potted form by first cooking, then boning, grinding up, seasoning and packing solid in 10-oz. cans, 2 dozen to the case, or 5-oz. cans, 4 dozen to the case. A combination of equal parts of chicken and beef tongue, potted together, is very popular; also, turkey and beef tongue; chicken and ham; turkey and ham. All kinds of fowl may be preserved by cooking and canning, either whole or boned. Canned boned chicken and turkey, in 1-℔. tins, are established articles in the market. The breast of large fowl, especially turkey or chicken, roasted and canned whole is very excellent. Fowl, which is intended to be canned without being boned, should be cooked thoroughly before going into the can.

GAME.

Game of all kinds is potted in the same manner as tongue and fowl, as described above. Packed in 10-oz. cans, 2 dozen to the case, or 5-oz. cans, 4 dozen to the case.

HAM.

Ham is potted, either alone and in the same manner as described above for tongue and fowl, or in combination with fowl, generally chicken or turkey, or with tongue. Packed in 10-oz. cans, 2 dozen to the case, or 5-oz. cans, 4 dozen to the case.

MUTTON.

Mutton is prepared for the can and packed in the manner described for fresh beef; it may be roasted or boiled.

Lamb's tongue is canned whole, after being well cooked. Packed in 1-℔. cans, 2 dozen to the case.

SUNDRIES.

Besides the above, pig's feet, spiced or not, tripe, soups of all kinds, plum pudding and other delicacies, are prepared ready to be served, then put into cans varying from 1-℔. to 5-℔. Indeed any kind of food, whether fruit, vegetable, fish or meat, or any combination of these may be prepared to suit the taste and ready to be served, then preserved for years in hermetically sealed tins and other vessels, provided the packages are carefully exhausted, securely sealed or "tipped" and well processed.

---

(2)

PROCESS.

NOTE.—We give only one "Process" for meats, which will answer for all kinds, varying the time according to the size of the can. The time needed in processing is short because the meats are *already well cooked.*

Exhaust small cans, up to 3-℔., 10 minutes at 212°.

Exhaust large cans, up to 6-℔., 15 minutes at 212°.

Exhaust 14-℔. cans 20 minutes at 212°.

Closed-top: for 5-oz. and 10-oz. cans, allow process of 5 minutes at 240°.

Closed-top: for 1-℔. and 2-℔. cans allow process of 10 minutes at 240°.

Closed-top : for 3-℔. cans allow process of 15 minutes at 240°.

Closed-top : for 4-℔. cans allow process of 18 minutes at 240°.

Closed-top : for 5-℔. cans allow process of 22 minutes at 240°.

Closed-top : for 14-℔. cans allow process of 45 minutes at 240°.

VII.

CAPPING SOLDER, &c.—THE MAR-KETS FOR CANNED GOODS.

CAPPING SOLDER.

No. 1 is composed of 100 parts lead, 100 parts tin.
No. 2 is composed of 100 parts lead, 90 parts tin.
No. 3 is composed of 100 parts lead, 80 parts tin.
No. 4 is composed of 100 parts lead, 70 parts tin.

No solder containing less than 70 parts tin to 100 parts lead should be used in capping cans. Solder-hemmed caps are now coming into favor, many packers using them in preference to the plain caps and solder.

SOLDERING FLUID.

Soldering fluid for preparing surfaces to be soldered, without the use of resin or similar substance, can be had. A barrel of this fluid contains about 50 gallons and will cap about 200,000 cans; but it can be bought in any desired quantities, from 1 gallon to 50 gallons, and at small cost. A good substitute for the above is easily made thus: take a convenient quantity of muriatic acid and add to it slowly particles of zinc till bubbles cease to to rise, and then add sal-ammoniac at the rate of 6 oz. to each gallon of acid. With this acid, however, resin, or something similar, must be used in soldering.

CASES.

We have already given the number of cans of the various sizes that are usually packed in a case, and the packer can easily compute the sizes of the cases that he needs, if he wishes to make his own cases. If he orders them of a box-maker he will simply have to specify in the order what size, and how many cans, are to be packed in a case. It is generally better to order cans and cases from the same party for then the cans can be put into the cases and both shipped to better advantage. If, however, the cases are ordered without the cans they should be ordered in the " shook " or knocked-down form. They cost considerably less, delivered, this way, take up less room at the canning house and can be easily and quickly set up when needed.

STENCILS.

Stencils are necessary for branding cases after packing. They are made from sheet metal, usually brass, and can be had of any design and cost but little.

THE MARKETS FOR CANNED GOODS.

The great canned goods markets in the United States are New York, Chicago, Baltimore, San Francisco, Boston and Philadelphia. New York leads, being a general market for goods from all parts of the country; then comes Chicago, the centre of the great meat-packing business and also the distributing point for the whole West; next comes Baltimore, the centre of the fine vegetable, fruit and oyster canning industry of the East; then San Francisco, that controls two-thirds of the Salmon output besides being the point from which the fine canned fruits of the Pacific coast are shipped East; then Boston, the centre of the great marine fish-canning industry and the general market for the New England states; then Philadelphia, as a general market.

Many others are also markets for canned goods, but the above are the recognized centres and distributing points. Many large jobbing houses in these places control to a very great extent the output of neighboring canning factories, while others have their own factories or contract with factories to supply them, buying up the entire output for future delivery.

It may often happen that packers who are remote from the large markets can dispose of their goods to better advantage in the smaller markets nearer home; this is more likely to be the case with those whose output is small. For the benefit of those who are thus situated we give below a list of good local markets for various sections of country.

For Virginia we would recommend Richmond.

For North Carolina we would recommend Wilmington.

For South Carolina we would recommend Charleston.

For Georgia we would recommend Atlanta, Augusta or Savannah.

For Florida we would recommend Jacksonville.

For Alabama we would recommend Mobile, Birmingham or Montgomery.

For Mississippi we would recommend New Orleans, St. Louis or Kansas City.

For Louisiana we would recommend New Orleans or St. Louis.

For Missouri we would recommend St. Louis or Kansas City.

For Texas we would recommend Galveston or St. Louis.

For Tennessee we would recommend Chattanooga, Nashville or Cincinnati.

For Kentucky we would recommend Louisville or Cincinnati.

For Ohio we would recommend Cincinnati or Cleveland.

For the Northwest we would recommend St. Paul and Milwaukee in addition to Chicago, which is the great Canned Goods Market for the whole West, Northwest and Pacific Coast. In the above markets packers can find commission brokers and jobbers to handle their product. In the principal markets brokers are to be found who handle canned goods exclusively, and generally these are to be recommended as looking out for the packer's best interest because they have no interest but the packer's, and therefore obtain the very highest market prices.

VIII.

APPENDIX.

CANNED GOODS LAW OF MARYLAND.

APPROVED BY THE GOVERNOR, APRIL 7, 1886.

SECTION 1. *Be it enacted by the General Assembly of Maryland,* That it shall be unlawful in this State for any packer of or dealer in hermetically canned or preserved fruits, vegetables or articles of food (excepting oysters), to sell such canned or preserved fruits, vegetables or other articles of food aforesaid, unless the cans, jars, or vessels which contain the same, shall bear the name and address of the person, firm or corporation, that canned or packed the article, or the name of the dealer who purchases the same from the packer or his agent, such name and address shall be plainly printed on the label in letters not less than three-sixteenths of an inch in height and one-eighth of an inch in breadth, together with a brand mark or term, indicating clearly the grade or quality of the article contained therein.

SEC. 2. *And be it enacted,* That all packers and dealers in "Soaked Goods," put up from products dried or cured before canning or sealing shall in addition to complying with the provisions of section one of this Act, cause to be printed plainly diagonally across the face of the label in good legible type, one half of an inch in height and three-eighths of an inch in width the words "Soaked Goods."

SEC. 3. *And be it enacted,* Any person, firm or corporation violating any of the provisions of this act shall be deemed guilty of a misde-

121

meanor and fined not less than fifty dollars nor more than one thousand dollars to be recovered by indictment in any court in this State having criminal jurisdiction, one-half of said fine to be paid to the informer and the other half to the State Treasury as other fines are paid.

SEC. 4.   This Act shall take effect from November 1, 1886.

NEW YORK CANNED GOODS BILL.

CHAPTER 369.

AN ACT in relation to canned or preserved food. Passed May 12, 1885; three-fifths being present. The people of the State of New York, represented in Senate and Assembly, do enact as follows :

SECTION 1.   It shall hereafter be unlawful in this state for any packer of or dealer in hermetically sealed canned or preserved fruits, vegetables or other articles of food to sell or offer such canned or preserved articles for sale, for consumption in this State after January 1st, eighteen hundred and eighty-six, unless the cans or jars which contain the same shall bear the name, address and place of business of the person, firm or corporation that canned or packed the article so offered, or the name of the wholesale dealer in this State who sells or offers the same for sale; together in all cases with the name of the state, county and city, town or village, where the same were packed, plainly printed thereon, preceded by the words " Packed at." Such name, address and place of business shall be plainly printed on the label, together with a mark or term indicating clearly the grade or quality of the article contained therein.

SEC. 2.   All packers of and dealers in soaked goods or goods put up from products dried or cured before canning shall in addition to complying with the provisions of section one of this act, cause to be plainly branded on the face of the label in good legible type, one-half of an inch in height and three-eighths of an inch in width, the word " Soaked."

SEC. 3.   All goods packed prior to the passage of this act, and all goods imported or to be imported from foreign countries of foreign manufacture are exempted from the provision of this act.

SEC. 4. Any packer or dealer who shall violate any of the provisions of this act shall be deemed guilty of a misdemeanor, and punished by a fine of not more than $50 for each offense in the case of retail dealers, and in the case of wholesale dealers and packers by a fine of not less than $500 nor more than $1,000 for each offense. The terms "packer" and "dealer" as used in this act shall be deemed to include any firm or corporation doing business as a dealer in or packer of the articles mentioned in this act. It shall be the duty of any board of health in this state cognizant of any violation of this act to prosecute any person, firm or corporation which it has any reason to believe has violated any of the provisions of this act, and the court or officer receiving the fine under any conviction under this act, after deducting the cost of trial and conviction, shall pay the same over to the board of health prosecuting the case. In case such offense is not prosecuted by any board of health the fine received shall be disposed of in the manner now provided by law.

SHELL OYSTER MEASURING LAW OF MARYLAND.

CHAPTER 281.

AN ACT to repeal chapter four hundred and fifty-six of the acts of the General Assembly of Maryland passed at the session of eighteen hundred and eighty-six, entitled "An act authorizing the governor to appoint general measurers of oysters for the State of Maryland," and to re-enact the same with amendments, and to designate the licensed measurers of oysters.

SECTION 1. *Be it enacted by the General Assembly of Maryland,* That chapter four hundred and fifty-six of the acts passed at the January session of eighteen hundred and eighty-six, entitled "An act to repeal chapter two hundred and ninety-nine of the acts passed at the session of eighteen hundred and eighty-four, entitled 'An act authorizing the governor to appoint general measurers of oysters for the State of Maryland,'" be and the same is hereby repealed and the following enacted in lieu thereof for the better measurement of oysters sold in the shell in this State;

SEC. 2. *And be it enacted,* That the governor at each session of the general assembly, shall appoint five persons for the city of Baltimore, and one person for each of all the other ports or towns bordering upon the Chesapeake Bay and its tributaries, to be known as the general measurers of oysters for the city, town or port for which he shall be appointed. Each general measurer of oysters shall give bond to the State of Maryland in the sum of three thousand dollars for the faithful performance of his duties; and the general measurer of oysters shall have the same power and authority over oysters sold in the adjacent waters to the port for which he shall have been appointed as are hereinafter given to said general measurers over such city, town or port for which he is appointed.

SEC. 3. *And be it enacted,* That at the beginning of each oyster season the five general measurers of oysters for the city of Baltimore shall meet in said city and divide it into five oyster districts, to be known as the first, second, third, fourth and fifth districts of the city of Baltimore, so as to include all the territory where oysters are landed from boats or vessels in said city; and those general measurers of oysters shall weekly change districts, so that no general measurer of oysters shall act the second time in any one district until he has acted once in every other district.

SEC. 4. *And be it enacted,* That it shall be the duty of said general measurers of oysters to see that the measurers of oysters shall be licensed, as required by law; that they shall properly measure the oysters, and that the law in reference to the measurement of oysters be strictly complied with; and the general measurers of oysters shall have the authority at all times to enter all places and all vessels where oysters are being measured in the shell, and to inspect all the measurements or instruments used in measuring oysters; and if these measures are incorrect, the said general measurers of oysters shall take possession of the incorrect measures and prosecute in the name of the state the party or parties found using said incorrect measures; and the said general measurers of oysters are hereby authorized and empowered to arrest all party or parties violating any of the provisions of the law in reference to the measurement of oysters; and it shall be the duty of the judge of the court of common pleas of the city of Baltimore, or the judge of the circuit court of any of the counties of this State, upon petition of any of the general measurers of oysters alleging that any licensed measurer of oysters has been convicted of violating any of the provisions of the law of this State in reference to the measurement of oysters, and the production of the record or a copy thereof, of the court or justice of the peace where such conviction was had, to suppress the license of such licensed measurer; and no license shall be granted him for the remainder of the oyster season in which such license was suppressed; and it shall further be the duty of the general measurers of oysters, under oath, to return to the governor of the State annually the amount of oysters measured in the city, town or port for which he shall be appointed.

SEC. 5. *And be it enacted*, That the general measurers of oysters of Baltimore city, or a majority of them, are hereby empowered and authorized to suspend the right or privilege of any person licensed to measure oysters in said city, to so measure oysters under said license; provided, however, that no such right to suspend shall exist unless a charge is pending against said licensed measurer for a violation of the laws of this State in reference to the measurement of oysters; and if such charge shall be dismissed by a court of competent jurisdiction such suspension, if exercised by said general measurers of oysters, shall end, and the captain or owner of the vessel shall designate the measurer or licensed measurer to measure the oysters sold out of said vessels.

SEC. 6. *And be it enacted*, That the general measurers of oysters shall receive a compensation for the faithful performance of their duties of ten cents per hundred bushels, to be paid by the seller and collected for the general measurers of oysters; when oysters are sold by the cargo or wholesale, by the buyers, and when oysters are sold in quantity or retail, by the commission merchant selling such oysters; and any seller who shall refuse to pay such compensation and any buyer or commission merchant who shall refuse to collect and pay over any such compensation to the said general measurers of oysters, as well as all other persons who shall violate any of the provisions of this act, or interfere with any of the general measurers of oysters in the discharge of their duties, upon conviction by any justice of the peace of this state, pay a fine of twenty dollars and costs; one-half of said fine to be paid to the informer, and in default of which such person or persons fined be confined in jail for a period not to exceed twenty days.

Sec. 7. *And be it enacted,* That all oysters measured in this State shall be measured either in a one-half bushel tub, a bushel tub, a bushel-and-one-half tub or a three bushel tub; and all instruments of measurements for measuring oysters in the shell shall be an iron circular tub with straight sides and straight solid bottom with holes in the bottom, if desired, for draining; such holes to be no larger, however than one inch in diameter. A half bushel tub shall have the following dimensions, all measurements to be from inside to inside, fifteen inches across the top, thirteen inches across the bottom, and seventeen inches diagonal from the inside chimb to the top; a bushel tub shall measure sixteen and one-half inches across at the bottom from inside to inside twenty-one inches diagonal from the inside chimb to the top, eighteen inches across from inside to inside at the top; a bushel-and-one-half tub shall measure nineteen inches across the top from inside to inside, eighteen inches across the bottom from inside to inside, and twenty-four inches from the inside chimb to the top; a three-bushel tub shall measure twenty-four inches across the top from inside to inside at the top, twenty-two inches from inside to inside at the bottom, and twenty-nine and twenty-six one hundredths inches from the inside chimb to the top; and and all oysters measured in the shell, as required by law, shall be even or struck measure; and any person or persons engaged in the business of buying or selling oysters in this State, who shall own or have in his possession any instrument of measurement for oysters which differs in size or description from the measures hereinbefore mentioned, with intent to use the same for measuring oysters, shall be guilty of a misdemeanor, and punished accordingly by a court of competent jurisdiction; all tubs to be stamped by the proper officer of the locality where such tubs are used.

Sec. 8. *And be it enacted,* That in addition to the charges herein mentioned for compensation to the general measurers of oysters, it shall be unlawful for the buyer of any cargo or part of a cargo of oysters sold in the shell to exact of or retain from the proceeds of said cargo or part of a cargo due the seller, a larger or greater sum or amount than one cent per bushel, in which shall be included the amount now allowed by law to be paid by the seller to the licensed measurer, and any person or persons charging or exacting a larger sum shall be subject to a fine of fifty dollars upon conviction before any justice of the peace, one-half of said fine to be paid to the informer.

SEC. 9. *And be it enacted,* That this act shall take effect from the date of its passage.

SHUCKED OYSTER MEASURING LAW OF MARYLAND.

CHAPTER 303.

AN ACT, to Fix the Standard of the Measurement of Shucked Oysters in All Oyster Houses in the State of Maryland.

SECTION 1. *Be it enacted by the General Assembly of Maryland,* That all Shucked Oysters opened at any oyster house in this State, or sold or delivered to any proprietors of any such Oyster House, to be shipped in any line of transportation to the customers of said proprietors, shall be shucked by the gallon and not by the can or vessel of any other name and designation, and it shall not be lawful for any such proprietor to contract with any person to shuck or open oysters at any such house, or for the proprietor thereof for the purpose aforesaid, otherwise than by the gallon.

SEC. 2. *And be it enacted,* That the said Oyster Houses, or the proprietors thereof, may use the regular Standard Wine Gallon Measure, or in consideration of the quantity of water contained in Shucked Oysters, the said houses or their proprietors may use a cup, which is hereby declared and determined to be an "Oyster Gallon Cup," which shall contain nine pints, Wine Measure, and no more; and no other than the Standard Wine Gallon Measure or said "Oyster Gallon Cup," shall be used in said houses, or by the proprietors thereof, in measuring any oysters to be shipped therefrom or used in the business of said houses, or the proprietor thereof; and said "Oyster Gallon Cup" shall be inspected and stamped by the same officer in the city of Baltimore or in any of the counties of the State, as is now required by law to inspect and stamp the wine gallon measure, and the persons neglecting to have the same stamped and inspected shall be subject to the same fines and penalties as are now or may hereafter be prescribed by law, for neglecting to have inspected and stamped the wine gallon measure; and any person using any other measure than above prescribed in any oyster house in this State, or any proprietor of any of said oyster houses, using any other than the above prescribed measures to measure any oysters to be shipped by him or used in his business, shall be guilty of a misdemeanor, and on conviction thereof before any Justice of the Peace of said county shall be fined not less than ten nor more than one hundred dollars in the discretion of the Justice, and shall stand committed until fine and costs are paid; one-half of said fine shall be paid to the State of Maryland and one half to the informer; but the person so convicted shall have the right of appeal as now provided by law in other criminal cases.

Approved April 7, 1886.

LIST OF PACKERS OF HERMETICALLY SEALED GOODS IN THE UNITED STATES.

Alphabetically arranged according to States and Towns.

(1.) FRUITS AND VEGETABLES.

ALABAMA.

Batesville, Barbour Canning Co.
Birmingham, Southern Pickling
and Manufacturing Co.
Florence, Florence Canning Co
Huntsville, Hicks, G. E.
La Fayette, Oliver, E. M.
Mentone, Mentone Canning Co.
Tredegar, Tredegar Canning Co.
Tuskagee, Motley, J. J.
Cox and Barrow.

ARKANSAS.

Arkansas City, Arkansas City
Canning Co.
Boonsboro, Boonsboro C'g Co.
Clarksville, Clarksville C'g Co.
Fort Smith, Fort Smith C'g Co.
Harrison, Harrison Canning Co.
Judsonia, Judsonia Canning Co.
Monticello, Drew County C'g Co.

Ozark, Ozark Canning Co.
Prairie Grove, Butler & Butler.
Prairie Grove Canning Co.
Rodgers, Rodgers Canning Co.
Russelville, Russelville C'g Co.
Springdale, Springdale C'g Co.
Van Buren, Van Buren, C'g Co.
West Fork, West Fork C'g Co.

CALIFORNIA.

Banning, Banning Canning Co.
Benicia, Benicia Packing Co.
Carquinez Packing Co.
Chico, Ranco Chico Canning Co.
Collinsville, Sacramento River
Canning Co.
Colton, Colton Canning Co.
Minor, A. A.
Eel River, Pacific Coast P'g Co.
Eureka, Humbolt Packing Co.
Fresno, Fresno Packing Co.
Gilroy, Gilroy Packing Co.

9   129

Healdsburg, Magnolia C'g Co.
    Van Al'en Packing Co.
    Windsor Packing Co.
Los Angeles, German Fruit Co.
    Southern Cal. Packing Co.
Los Gatos, Los Gatos Packing Co.
Martenez, Cutting Packing Co.
    Martenez Canning Co.
Marysville, Marysville C'g Co.
Napa, Toole, S. M.
Oakland, Lusk, J., Canning Co.
Petaluma, Petaluma Canning Co.
Pomona, Pomona Canning Co.
Riverside, King Morse C'g Co.
    Newberry, J. R., & Co.
    Passadena Canning Co.
Sacramento, Capitol Packing Co.
San Francisco, Antiguez C'g Co.
    Banner Packing Co.
    Capital Packing Co.
    Cole, Elfelt & Co.
    Coleman, Wm. T. & Co.
    Columbus Packing Co.
    Cutting Packing Co.
    Fisher Packing Co.
    Fontana & Co.
    Golden Gate Packing Co.
    Nicholas Goetjen.
    Hume, G. W.
    King Morse Canning Co.
    Lusk, A., & Co.
    Meade, G. W., & Co.
    Merry, Faull & Co.
    Overland Packing Co.
    Pike, C. W.
    San José Fruit Packing Co.
    Schammel & Co.
    Scotchler & Gibbs.
    Wagenheim, S., & Co.
    Wyland & Co.
San José, California Packing Co.
    Dawson, J. M., Packing Co.
    Flickinger, J. H.
    Garden City Packing Co.
San Lorenzo, Lusk, A., C'g Co.
    Golden Gate Packing Co.
    Lusk, A., & Co.
    San José Packing Co.

Santa Clara, Meade, G. W., & Co.
Santa Cruz, Santa Cruz P'g Co.
Santa Rosa, Cutting Packing Co.
    Santa Rosa Packing Co.
South Valejo, The Benicia P'g Co.
Whittier, Whittier Canning Co.
Winters, Winters Canning Co.
Yuba City, Sutter Canning Co.

COLORADO.

Boulder, Boulder Canning Co.
Brighton, Brighton Canning Co.
Canon City, Canon City C'g Co.
Denver, Butters Canning Co.
Marquis, Küner P'g and Pickling
    Co.
    Marquis Canning Co.
Little, Little Packing Co.
Longmont, Empson Packing Co.

CONNECTICUT.

Deep River, Conn. Valley C'g Co.
Guilford, Sachem Head C'g Co.
Middleton, Stiles & Parker Pre-
    serving Co.
New Haven, Merriam & Son.
    New Haven Preserving Co.
New London, Pequot Preserving
    Co.
Trumbull, Trumbull Canning Co.

DELAWARE.

Bridgeville, Clark Canning Co.
Camden, Stelson, Ellison & Co.
Clayton, Smith & Carsons.
Delaware City, Anderson Pre-
    serving Co.
    Beck & Pancoast.
    Campbell & Anderson.
Dover, J. M. Chambers P'g Co.
    Richardson & Robbins.
Ellendale, Jester & Reed.
Felton, Clifton & Co.
    Jas. T. Farrell.
    G. H. Killen & Co.

Fredericka, McNitt Canning Co.
McNitt & Hydon.
Reik, H. A., & Co.
Reynolds & Postells.
Rodgers, C. P.
Rodgers, A. C.
Georgetown, Calhoun & Thorough-
good.
Macklin, S. H., & Co.
Greenwood, Short, J. E., & Co.
Harrington, Reed, J. C.
Houston, Counselman, J. B., & Co.
Houston Canning Co.
Johnson, G.
Kenton, Armstrong & Co.
Laurel, Laurel Canning Co.
Smith & Co.
Leipsic, Levin's, S. H., Sons.
Lincoln, Small & Son.
Middleton, Arthur, H. L.
Clayton, Briggs & Co.
Maxwell, J. B.
Wells & Harrington.
Milford, Davis, R. H.
Harris & Co.
Jenkins, S. T.
Thompson & Hill.
Milton, Reynolds & Co.
Odessa, Watkins Packing Co.
Port Penn, Dilworth & Stewart.
Rising Sun, Farmer's Preserving
Co.
Seaford, Stevens, W. H., & Co.
St. Georges, St. Georges C'g Co.
Smyrna, Hofleckes & Co.
Wilmington, Harvey & Sisler.
Franco-American Food Co.
Woodside, Anderson, T. P.
Derby, S. H., & Co.
Wyoming, Cornwell & Co.
Sullivan, B., & Co.
Wyoming Canning Co.

FLORIDA.

Callahan, Harris, W. S.
Campville, Campville C'g Co.
Fernandina, Bell River P'g Co.

Fort Myers, Fort Myers C'g Co.
Gainesville, Bowling. Parker.
Huntington, Henderson, J. A.
Milton, Milton Canning Co.
Ocala, Anderson, W. L.
Oxford, Oxford Canning Co.
Plant City, Eureka Canning Co.
Silver Springs, Silver Springs C'g
Co.
St. Augustine, St. Augustine C'g
and Preserving Co.
Starke, Starke Canning Co.

GEORGIA.

Adairsville, Adairsville C'g Co.
Augusta, Augusta Canning Co.
Brunswick, Downing, C., & Co.
Camilla, Camilla Canning Co.
Cartersville, Milan, C. M., & H. M.
Dalton, North Georgia C'g Co.
Eastman, Eastman Canning Co.
Eatonton, Putnam County C'g Co.
Forsythe, Forsythe Canning Co.
Griffin, Griffin Canning Co.
Jackson, Jackson Canning Co.
Macon, Macon Canning Co.
Outler, Harris & Co.
Marshallville, Marshallville C'g
Co.
Montezuma, Montezuma C'g Co.
Milledgeville, Milledgeville C'g
Co.
Ringgold, Ringgold Canning Co.
Sparta, Brown, A. E.

ILLINOIS.

Bloomington, Bloomington C'g Co.
Bushnell, Bushnell Canning Co.
Carrollton, Carrollton P'g Co.
Centralia, Centralia Canning Co.
Chester, Chester Canning Co.
Chicago, Booth, A., Packing Co.
Hately Bros.
Lawler, C. A.
National C'g and Preserving
Co.

Chicago, Reiber Preserving Co.
   Tobey & Booth.
   Weber, C. M., & Co.
   West, J. R.
Chillicothe, Chillicothe C'g Co.
Dixon, Fargo, F. N.
Effingham, Effingham C'g Co.
Elgin, Elgin Packing Co.
Elmwood, Elmwood Packing Co.
Freeport, Freeport Canning Co.
Gibson City, Gibson City C'g Co.
Galena, Crummer & Meller.
Geneva, Alexander, H. B.
Hoopestown, Hoopestown C'g Co.
   Illinois Canning Co.
Jerseyville, Smith & Son.
Kansas, Staff Bros. & Co.
Lacon, Lacon Canning Co.
La Moille, La Moille Canning Co.
Lewiston, College City C'g Co.
   Ranny, Doty & Phelps.
Normal, Champion, T. E.
Olney, Olney Canning Co.
Pana, Van Derwater & Son.
Paxton, Paxton Canning Co.
Quincy, Berry E., & Son.
   Quincy Canning Co.
Salem, Salem Packing Co.
Sibley, Sibley Canning Co.
Sparta, Borders, W. R., & Son.
   Sparta Canning Co.
Sterling, Rock River Packing Co.
   Sterling Packing Co.
Sycamore, Sycamore Preserving
   Co.
Urbana, Urbana Canning Co.
Virginia, Virginia Packing Co.

INDIANA.

Columbus, Ruddick, B. S.
Evansville, Indiana Canning Co.
Flat Rock, Flat Rock Canning Co.
Fort Wayne, Angel, C.
Indianapolis, Adams & Sherman.
   Henry, T. L, & Co.
   Van Camp Packing Co.
Kokoma, Kokoma Canning Co.

Madison, Madison Canning Co.
North Manchester, North Man-
   chester Canning Co.
Oaktown, Oaktown Canning Co.
Princeton, Princeton Canning Co.
Whiteland, Whiteland C'g Co.

IOWA.

Astor, Astor Canning Co.
Atlantic, Atlantic Canning Co.
Boonesboro, Boone County Pack-
   ing Co.
Cedar Falls, Cedar Falls C'g Co.
Council Bluffs, Council Bluffs Can-
   ning Co.
Davenport, Davenport C'g Co.
Elgin, Elgin Canning Co.
Eldora, Alvord & Forker.
Fairfield, Fairfield Canning Co.
Gilman, Gilman Canning Co.
   Marshall Canning Co.
Glenwood, Glenwood Canning Co.
Indianola, Indianola Canning Co.
Keokuk, Anderson, F. M.
   Keokuk Canning Co.
La Mot, La Mot Canning Co.
Marshalltown, Marshall C'g Co.
   Marshall Preserving Co.
Muscatine, Muscatine Island Can-
   ning Co.
   Muscatine Royal Canning Co.
Newton, Newton Canning Co.
Shenandoah, Shenandoah C'g Co.
Sioux City, Sioux City C'g Co.
Vilesca, Vilesca Canning Co.
Vinton, Vinton Canning Co.
   Watson Canning Co.
Wapello, Wapello Canning Co.
Waverly, Waverly Canning Co.

KANSAS.

Abelene, Long, J. H., & Co.
Atchison, Sheppard, Jager & Co.
Belle Plain, Belle Plain P'g Co.
Birmingham, Birmingham Can-
   ning Co.

Burlingame, Van Horn & Son.
Cornic Grove, Cornic Grove Canning Co.
Emporia, Emporia Canning Co.
Frederick, Frederick Canning Co.
Garnet, Garnet Canning Co.
Independence, Independence Canning Co.
Iola, Niosho Valley Canning Co.
Junction City, Junction City Canning Co.
Lawrence, Lawrence Canning Co.
Leavenworth, Globe Canning Co.
McPherson, McPherson C'g Co.
Moline, Moline Canning Co.
Nortonsville, Nortonsville Canning Co.
Olathe, Olathe Canning Co.
Osage, Osage Packing Co.
Oskaloosa, Oskaloosa Canning Co.
Oswego, Oswego Packing Co.
Paola, Paola Canning Co.
Pleasanton, Pleasanton C'g Co.
Salina, Salina Canning Co.
Severy, Severy Canning Co.
Topeka, Topeka Canning Co.
Wetmore, Wetmore Canning Co.
Wichita, Price, Dearing & Co.
Willis, Willis Canning Co.
Wyandotte, Anstey, Geo., & Co.

KENTUCKY.

Elizabethtown, Elizabethtown Canning Co.
Henderson, Henderson C'g Co.
Louisville, Hatley Bros.
Newport, Challenge Packing Co.

LOUISIANA.

Baton Rouge, Feltus, H. J.
La Fayette, La Fayette C'g Co.
New Orleans, Booth, A., P"g Co.
Dunbar's, G. W., Sons.
Ruston, North Louisiana C'g Co.
Shreveport, Shreveport Canning & Evaporating Co.

MAINE.

Anson, Winslow Packing Co.
Auburn, New Gloucester P'g Co.
Belgrade, Taylor, J. C., & Son.
Berlin, Potter & Wrightington.
Bethel, Bethel Canning Co.
Bowdoinham, Bowdoinham Canning Co.
Seegars Bros.
Brooklyn, Brooklyn Canning Co.
Winslow Packing Co.
Brunswick, Jordan, F. C.
Camden, Winslow Packing Co.
Cape Elizabeth, Mitter, W. B.,
Cherryfield, Cherryfield P'g Co.
Stewart, A. L.
Columbia Falls, Columbia Falls Packing Co.
Cumberland Centre, Cumberland Packing Co.
Cumberland Junction, Cumberland Packing Co.
Deering, Winslow Packing Co.
Deer Isle, Potter & Wrightington.
Denmark, Burnham & Morrill.
Dexter, Moses Bros.
Moses, C. T.
Dixfield, Burnham & Morrill.
Durham, Durham Packing Co.
Fields, W. H.
East Hiram, Burnham & Morrill.
Winslow Packing Co.
Fairfield, Fairfield Corn C'g Co.
Winslow Packing Co.
Farmington, Sandy River P'g Co.
Titcomb, Hiram.
Waugh, Cothren & Williams.
Winslow Packing Co.
Gardner, Hamilton, J. E.
Garland, Hamilton, J. E.
Gillead, Gillead Canning Co.
Gorham, Branch Canning Co.
Johnson Canning Co.
North Branch Canning Co.
Portland Packing Co.
Green's Landing, Green's Landing Packing Co.

Green's Landing, Potter & Wrightington.
  Thurlow, Knowlton & Co.
Hallowell, Hallowell Packing Co.
  Union Packing Co.
Hope, True, L. P.
Jonesport, Jonesport Packing Co.
  Potter & Wrightington.
  Stimpson & Parker.
Knightville, Nutter Bros.
Leeds, Webb, H. F., & Co.
Lisbon, Merrill Bros.
Livermore Centre, Leavitt, L., & Son.
Livermore Falls, Gooding, E. S.
Machias, Burnham & Morrill.
Marshfield, Merrill, Chas. A.
Mechanic Falls, Minot P'g Co.
Millbridge, Winslow Packing Co.
  Wyman, J. & E. A.
Minot, Burnham & Morrill.
North Lubec, Lubec Packing Co.
North Turner, N'th Turner P'g Co.
North Wayne, Jenning Bros.
Oceanville, Potter & Wrightington.
  Wyman, J., & E. A.
Paris, Burnham & Morrell.
Poland, Poland Packing Co.
Portland, Baxter H. C.
  Burnham & Morrell.
  Jones, J. W.
  Maine Canning Co.
  Mattocks, C. P.
  Portland Canning Co.
  Red Brook Packing Co.
  Shaw, Hammond & Kearney.
  Thompson, Hall & Co.
  Union Packing Co.
  Webb, H. F., & Co.
  Webb, J. B., & Co.
  Winslow Packing Co.
Raymond, Winslow Packing Co.
Richmond Corners, Getcell, C. F.
Rumford, Webb, H. F., & Co.
Saccarappa, Knight, Joseph.
Scarboro, Burnham & Morrill.
Sebago Lake, Burnham & Morrill.
South Windham, McClellan, John.

Stroudwater, Red Brook P'g Co.
Turner, North Turner P'g Co.
Wells, Portland Packing Co.
West Farmington, Weatheren, E. R., & Sons.
White Rock, Wilson, E. M.
Wilton, Jones Canning Co.
Winterport, Winterport P'g Co.
Yarmouth, Yarmouth P'g Co.
  Winchester Packing Co.
Yarmouthville, York, O. F., & Co.

MARYLAND.

Aberdeen, Baker, C. W.
  Baker, G. A.
  Baker, J. B.
  Baker & Morgan.
  Bayliss, J. W.
  Bayliss, W. S.
  Bowen, W. H.
  Cole, J. F.
  Courtney & Cole.
  Finney, J. L., & Bro.
  Foard, A. R., & Bro.
  Hunter, C. A.
  Jewens, W. E.
  Kraus, Conrad.
  Michael, J. C., & Son.
  Michael, J. M.
  Osborn, C. B.
  Osborn, L. S.
  Silver, H. Z.
  Wells, Jas., & Son.
Abingdon, Moulsdale, Thos.
Baltimore, Aughinbaugh C'g Co.
  Barnes, Hanson P.
  Booth, A., Packing Co.
  Boyer, W. W., & Co.
  Brinkley, J. B., & Sons.
  Farren, J. S., & Co.
  Fleming & Co.
  Freeman & Shaw.
  Gibbs Preserving Co.
  Grecht, W., & Co.
  Griffith, R. C., & Co.
  Hemingway, H. F.
  Horn, John H.

Baltimore, Houghton Packing Co.
King, John.
Lanfair, H. S., & Co.
Lewis, J. W.
Ludington, J., & Co.
McGaw, Davis & Co.
McGrath, H. J., & Co.
Mallory, E. B., & Co.
Maltby, C. S.
Maryland Preserving Co.
Medford & Aubrey.
Miller Bros., & Co.
Moore & Brady.
Moore, Roberts & Co.
Myer, Thos. J., & Co.
Nunsen, Wm., & Sons.
Pearson, C. H., & Co.
Platt & Co.
Stansburg, J. E., & Sons.
Stone, B. M., & Bro.
Summers, C. G., & Co.
Wagner, The Martin, Co.
Winebrenner, P. F., & D. E.
Bethlehem, Messick, R. M.
Belair, Beall, J. P.
Coale & Richardson.
Lynch, D. P., Jr.
McGaw, C. A.
Martin, August.
Walker, Geo. F.
Whistler, E. B., & Bro.
Bentley's Springs, Jordan, J. C.
Boothby Hill, Aronson, W. F.
Calvary, Derickson, W. L.
Harvey, John.
Cambridge, Wallace, Jas., & Son.
Mace, Woolford & Co.
Canton, Adams, Michael.
Carsin's Run, Armstrong, G. S.
Baker, Nicholas.
Bicktold, Fred.
Bodt & Hanson.
Bonnett & Son.
Burkley & Smith.
Carsins, E. E.
Ellsener, John.
Gilbert, Benjamin.
Gilbert, M. M.

Carsin's Run, Jewens, Wm. E.
Maxwell, J. W.
Castleton, Knight, J. T., & Co.
Chase, Bramble J.
Chesapeake City, Hopper, T. B.
Chestertown, Rice, Lamotte & Co.
Choptank, Wright, J. A., & Bro.
Chrome Hill, Street, H. W.
Churchville, Baker, J. C.
Blackburn, C. O.
Burbank, Jesse.
Chestney, W. H.
Coale, J. F.
Coale, P. F.
Everest, Geo. H.
Hanson, D. H.
Johnson, S.
Martin, Geo. H.
Clayton, Archer, D. J.
Lehman Bros.
Cole, Mitchell, J. P., & Bro.
Conowingo, Adams, Sam.
Graham, E.
Cooperstown, Durham, W. A.
Creswell, Callahan, Pat.
Callahan, Dan.
Cullom, J. J.
Hanway, B. F.
Hamby, J. W.
McKee, D., & Son.
Webster, J. T.
Webster, R.
Darlington, Andrew, C. B.
Edge, E. S.
. Hopkins, E. C.
Hopkins, J. R.
Deer Creek, Silver, S. B.
Deer Park, Janney, J. H.
Denton, Reddon & Co.
Roe, H. A.
Dublin, Dieckman, H.
Forwood, L.
Jones, G. W.
Dunkirk, Calvert Canning Co.
Easton, Hubbard & Bro.
Wrightson, C. T.
East Newmarket, Lord, E. E.
Millard, B.

Edgewood, Gunther, Fred.
  Hanson & Lantz.
  Kimball, G. A., & Co.
Ellicott City, Herbert Bros.
Elk Neck, Crouch & White.
Emmorton, Amos, Isaac.
  Brevard, W. H., & Son.
  De Moss, J. M.
  Plowman, J. H., & Bro.
  Rodgers, E.
Fairmount, Miles & Cox.
Fallston, Hamilton, J. K.
  Robinson, A.
  Robinson, L. B.
Federalsburg, Goslin & Davis.
Federal Hill, Shambarger, Wm.
Forest Hill, Armstrong, John.
  Grafton, J. A.
  Grafton, Lee.
  Johnson, Jas. N.
Fork, Carty, S. R.
  Gorsuch, F. B.
Fountain Green, Harwood, C. W.
  Harwood, Wm. H.
  Wilkinson, H. M. & Bro.
  Wilkinson, T. M. & Son.
Frederick, McMurray P'g Co.
Garland, Wilkinson, G. A.
Glencoe, Lemmon, Geo. H.
Glenville, Silver, Ben.
Greensboro, Bernard, Joseph.
  Roe, A. B.
  Statterfield, W. C.
Hampstead, Shriver, J.
Harford Furnace, Callahan, J.
  Cullom, H. & Bro.
  Dalton & Sons.
  Griffin, J. W.
  Oliver & Son.
Havre de Grace, Brown, A. F.
  Evans, J. T. & Son.
  Hopper Bros.
  Jarrett, Gilbert.
  King, W. J.
  McGaw, Jas. W.
  McGaw, R. F.
  Silver, W. Z.
  Stansbury, Jas. E.

Havre de Grace, Ward, James.
Harman's, Shipley, H. L., & Bro.
Hebbville, Emmart Bros.
Hickory, Carcard, Thos.
  Forwood, W.
  Pyle, H.
Hurlocks, Wright, T. J.
Hyde's Station, Hyde & Son.
Jarrettsville, Gilbert, J. C.
Jessup's, Lowckamp, J. F.
Joppa, Cook, Jas., Jr.
  Hanway, J. B.
  Pyle, A.
Lauraville, List & Shultz.
Level, Baldwin, Geo.
  Baldwin Bros.
  Bowman, W. S., Jr.
  Ferrell, M.
  Hopkins, G. R., & Bro.
  Hopkins, J. E., & Bro.
  Kenley, J. F.
  Spencer, J. W.
  Walker, J. P.
  Walker, J. R.
  Walker, S. A., & Co.
Linkwood, Reed, J. M.
Loch Earn, Ridgely, H. C.
Locust, Boyle, Andrew.
Lynch, Bellingham, Jas.
Lyons Creek, Calvert Canning Co.
Magnolia, Brown & Harris.
  Hanway, J. B.
  Sweeting, Ed.
Manor, Barnes, R. A.
  Barnes, W. H.
Marion Station, Boulbourn Bros.
  Hall, H. W., & Son.
Marydell, Stemmer, F. G.
Michaelsville, Botts & Coale.
Mitchellsville, Davis, Joseph.
  Poula, Frank.
  Smith & Co.
Millgreen, Andrews, G. W.
  Andrews, Isaac.
  Barkus, C. W.
  Famous, A. J.
  Famous, J. W.
New Windsor, Boyle & Stouffer.

NewWindsor,NewWindsorC'gCo.
Norrisville, Edie, David A.
North East, Rutter & Thomas.
Oakwood, Bennett, J. J.
Odenton, Murray, Geo. M.
Oxford, Seth Canning Co.
Patapsco, Westaway, F. J.
Perryman's, Arthur, H. S.
   Cronin & Son.
   Foy, F. T.
   Gilbert, N. B.
   Hall, Andrew.
   Hallis & Matthews.
   Hopkins, J. H.
   Mitchell, L. & Bro.
   Nelson & Bro.
   Nelson, H. C.
   Raymond, S. W.
   Sweeting, Geo. W.
   Wells & Co.
Pikesville, Harrison, C. K.
Pleasantville, Keen & Walker.
Princess Anne, Dashiell, C. M.
Prospect, Day, Geo. W.
   Scarboro, A. H.
   Slee, C. C.
Pylesville, Harry, C. F., & Co.
   Wilson, Samuel.
Rawlins, Frost & Bro.
Ridgeley, Day Bros., & Co.
Rising Sun, Brown, G. W.
Riverton, Bradley, A. H.
Rossville, Gillespie, J. M.
Salisbury, Stratner, F.
Sandy Springs, Pigeon, Chas.
Sharon Station, Horner & Co.
St. James, Hutchins, Wm.
St. Michael's, Willis & Tyler.
Stepney, Bellingham, Wm.
   Wells, J. M., & Bro.
Streets, Robertson, I.
Sudlersville, Gadd & Sudler.
Sweet Air, Stansbury, G. N.
Taylor, Emory, Dr. R.
   Rutledge, C. A.
The Rocks, Spenser, S. L.
Timonium, Warfield, S. Davies.
Triumph, Herald, Geo.

Tunis Mills, Smith, T. H.
Two Johns, Howard, Chas., &
   Son.
Upper Falls, Miller, A. A., & Co.
Vail, Klinefelter Bros.
   Robinson & Bros.
Vienna, Houston, Dr. J. H.
Waterbury, Baldwin, Richard.
Webster, Anderson, Geo.
   Briney, J. E.
   Evans, A. W. & W. E.
   Evans, John T.
   Preston, A.
   Preston & Bro.
   Preston, Benjamin.
   Preston, Jas. H.
Westminster, Shriver, B. F., & Co.
   Smith, Yingling & Co.
West River, Murray & Calhoun.
Whaleysville, Hammond & Bro.
Whiteford, Ellwood, H. W.
   Say, J. C.
   Whiteford, Jos. S.
   Whiteford, W. S.
Whitehall, Black & Co.
Wilna, Archer, G.
   Hollingsworth, A. B.
   Price, J. R.
Woodlawn, Rutter, J. T.

MASSACHUSETTS.

Boston, Huckins, J. H. W., & Co.
   Knight, A. A.
   Mayo Bros.
   New England Preserving Co.
   Pickert, L., & Co.
   Plummer, J. P. & D.
   Potter & Wrightington.
   Spurr, H. B., & Co.
   Underwood, Wm., & Co.
City Mills, Fisher, J. L.
Danvers, Gardner, J. Frank.
Medway, Hodges, W. B.
Northfield, Webster, L. T.
Provinceton, Pickert, L. & Co.
Somerville, Emerson, Geo. R.

MICHIGAN.

Adrian, Adrian Packing Co.
   Ladd, L.
   Lambin & Corbin.
   Riverside Canning Co.
Battle Creek, Howes, G. C.
Bay City, Bay City Canning Co.
Benton Harbor, Alden C'g Co.
   Eldred, N. J.
Cheyboygan, Mallory, D. H.
Detroit, Daley Preserving Co.
   Schroeder, V.
Dryden, Darwood & Lamb.
Hillsdale, Hillsdale Canning Co.
Holland, Holland Canning Co.
Howell, Howell Canning Co.
Jefferson, Hillsdale Canning Co.
Kalamazoo, Williams, J. & Son.
Lowell, Lowell Canning Co.
Oceana, Oceana Canning Co.
Owosso, Owosso Canning Co.
Pentwater, Anderson, Jno.
Quincy, Pressel & Lyon.
Three Rivers, Three Rivers Canning Co.

MINNESOTA.

Austin, Austin Canning Co.
Farabault, Farabault Canning Co.
Mankato, Mankato Canning Co.
Owatonna, Owatonna Canning Co.

MISSISSIPPI.

Beauregard, McIntosh, Frank.
Biloxi, Lopez, Dunbar's Sons & Co.
   Maybury, J. T.
   Sea Coast Packing Co.
Canton, Canton Canning Co.
Crystal Springs, Crystal Springs Canning Co.
Garden City, Mitchell, J. C.
Meridian, Meridian Canning Co.
Monticello, Monticello C'g Co.
Natchitoches, Breda, J. E.

New Albany, New Albany C'g Co.
Rienzi, Bullard, J. M.
Vicksburg, Vicksburg C'g Co.
West Point, Henderson, Jno.

MISSOURI.

Carthage, Carthage Canning Co.
   McGannon & Fay P'g Co.
Felton, Davis & Rankin.
Hamilton, Hamilton Canning Co.
Hardin, Missouri Valley C'g Co.
Higginsville, Chaney Canning Co.
   Shell City Canning Co.
Kansas City, Alcutt Packing Co.
   Keepers, Jno., & Co.
Kahokia, Kahokia, Canning Co.
Keydaysville, Keydaysville C'g Co.
Lexington, Silver Canning Co.
Nevada, Nevada Canning Co.
Norborn, Missouri Canning Co.
   Norborn Canning Co.
Pierce City, Pierce City C'g Co.
Pleasant Hill, Pleasant Hill C'g Co.
Republic, Republic Canning Co.
Rich Hill, Rich Hill C'g Co.
St. Joseph, St. Joseph C'g Co.
   Whiteford, Horace.
St. Louis, Hurst Packing Co.
   Mound City Preserving Co.
   St. Louis Can and C'g Co.
Warrensburg, Warrensburg C'g Co.
Willow Springs, Willow Springs Canning Co.

NEBRASKA.

Arapahoe, Arapahoe C'g Co.
Beatrice, Beatrice Canning Co.
Beemer, Beemer Canning Co.
Belair, Belair Canning Co.
Bloomington, Bloomington C'g Co.
Brock, Brock Canning Co.
Edgar, Edgar Canning Co.

Exeter, Exeter Canning Co.
Falls City, Falls City C'g Co.
  Waltmeyer & Son.
Fremont, Fremont Canning Co.
Grand Island, Grand Island C'g
  Co.
Kearney, Kearney Canning Co.
Nebraska City, Nebraska City
  Canning Co.
Niobrara, Niobrara Canning Co.
Plattsmouth, Caruth, F., & Co.
  Plattsmouth Canning Co.
Scotia, Scotia Canning Co.
Seward, Seward Canning Co.
Takamah, Takamah Canning Co.
Waterloo, Waterloo Canning Co.
Warnersville, Warnersville C'g
  Co.
West Lincoln, Lincoln C'g Co.
York, York Canning Co.

NEW HAMPSHIRE.

Bethel, Wyman Canning Co.
East Barrington, Dyer, Soule & Co.
  East Barrington Canning Co.

NEW JERSEY.

Alloway, Anderson, W. L.
Bordentown, Aaronson, R. H., &
  Co.
  Woerner, D. C., & Co.
Bridgeton, Ayars, B. S.
  Brady, J. F., & Co.
  Cox, I. H., & Co.
  Cumberland Packing Co.
  Probasco & Lanning.
Burlington, Birkmire, W. H.
  Cooper, W. H.
  Kirby Bros.
  Kirby, C. B.
Camden, Anderson Preserving Co.
  Campbell, Jos., & Co.
Canton, Sheppard, Jno P.
Cedarville, Deament, J. T.
  South Jersey Packing Co.
  Stevens, W. L.

Columbus, Aaronson, Harvey & Co.
Daretown, Kiger & Colson.
  Richman, Wm.
East Orange, Franco-American
  Food Co.
Egg Harbor City, Egg Harbor
  City Canning Co.
  Gardner, J. P.
  Kraus, Chas., & Son.
  Schwinghammer, Jno.
Elizabeth, Earl, C. B. & W. A. C.
Elmer, Smith, L. F.
Englishtown, Evans, H. C.
  Quackenbush, J. N.
Fairton, Stevens & Camm.
Freehold, Brakeley, Jos.
Greenwich, Bacon, Jos.
  Maull, B. F., & Co.
Hights Town, Chamberlain &
  Hutchison.
Keyport, Austin, Nichols & Co.
  Bucklin, C. S., & Co.
Lambertville, Butterfoss, J. H.
Manasquan, Stout, Wm. W.
Matawan, Bucklin, C. S., & Co.
Moorestown, Thurber, Wyland &
  Co.
New Egypt, Genet, John A.
Newport, Statheren, Cosier & Co.
Phalanx, Kuebler, John.
Pennsville, Bassett & Fogg.
Penns Grove, Hughes, R. D.
  Summerville & Co.
Quinton, Fogg & Hiers.
  Kelty, S. L.
Red Bank, Bucklin, J. & W. S.
  Oliver, P.
  Stout, John W.
Riverside, Cump, D.
  Leggett, Francis H., & Co.
Salem, Bassett Bros.
  Jones & Ayars.
  Myers & Hilliard.
  Starr & Bro.
  Waddington & Holme.
Sharptown, Richman, H. B.
Shrewsbury, Broadmeadow, Jas
  Hazzard, E. C., & Co.

Trenton, Grant & Dunn.
Wenonah, Devell & Perry.
Williamstown, The Sharp C'g Co.
Woodstown, Dickson & Lippincott.
 Farmers' Coöperative C'g Co.
Yorktown, Elwell, Jnò. S.

NEW YORK.

Adams, Webster, F. L.
Albany, Stevens, J. & Son.
Batavia, Batavia Preserving Co.
 Sprague, Warner & Co.
Blossvale, Blossvale Canning Co.
Brant, Erie Preserving Co.
Buffalo, Buffalo Conserve Co.
 Erie Preserving Co.
 N. Y. State Preserving Co.
Camden, Camden Canning Co.
 Hairland, L. P.
 Phelps & Co.
 Stoddard, G.
 Walker, J. E.
 Wood, J.
Cape Vincent, Cleveland, A. B. & Co.
Cherry Creek, Chautauqua Canning Co.
Clyde, Hemingway, M.
 Van Tassel, A. L.
Coxsackie, Lounsbury, E. H. & Co.
East Aurora, East Aurora Canning Co.
Eden, Eden Preserving Co.
Elmira, Westcnelt Bros.
Farnham, Erie Preserving Co.
Forestville, Curtiss, A. H.
 Forestville Canning Co.
 Tower, P.
Fredonia, Fredonia Canning Co.
Franklinville, Franklinville Canning Co.
Geneva, Geneva Canning Co.
Glencove, Hudson & Co.
Glenhead, Scudder & Townsend.
Goshen, Reed & Carnie.
Hamburg, Hamburg Canning Co.

Kenwood, Oneida Packing Co.
Lockport, Lawton Preserving Co.
 Niagara Preserving Co.
Long Island City, Bridge & Gregory.
Middleport, Ontario Preserving Co.
McConnellsville, Tuttle, Lansing & Co.
Mt. Morris, Revere Canning Co.
 Sweet & Co.
 Winters & Prophet.
New Hartford, New Hartford C'g Co.
Newport, Newport Canning Co.
New York, Austin, Nichols & Co.
 Erie Preserving Co.
 Franco-American Food Co.
 Gordon & Dilworth.
 Hemingway & Co.
 Kemp, Day & Co.
 Leggett, F. H., & Co.
 New York Desiccating Co.
 Ritter Conserve Co.
 Schimmel, O. O.
 Stout, Jno. W.
 Sutherland, Eugene.
 Thurber, H. K.
 Thurber, Wyland & Co.
North Collins, Western New York Preserving Co.
Orchard Park, Hamburg C'g Co.
Rochester, Burlingame & Bro.
 Clark, W. N.
 Curtice Bros.
Rome, Fort Stanwix Canning Co.
 Jones & Hower.
 Olney & Fowler.
 Rome Canning Co.
Roslyn, Hewlett, S. R.
Springville, Springville C'g Co.
Syracuse, Loomis & Sadler.
 Merrill & Soule.
 Patterson, F.
 Sycamore Canning Co.
 Windholtz, Louis.
Taberg, Loveland, P. G.
 White Bros.

Taberg, Wilson Canning Co.
Turin, Turin C'g & Pickling Co.
Utica, Floyd, Daniel G.
Verona, Bishop, T. B.
 Oneida County Canning Co.
Watkins, Cuykendall, J. W.
Webster, Darling, A. B.
 Webster Preserving Co.
Westfield, Westfield Canning Co.
Westernville, Olney & Floyd.
Williamstown, White, H. A.

NORTH CAROLINA.

Asheville, Asheville Canning Co.
Biltmore, Reed, M. L.
Burgaw, Farmer's Alliance Canning Co.
Carthage, Dockery, A. V.
Durham, Durham Canning Co.
Elizabeth City, Willis & Fleming.
Fayetteville, Fayetteville C'g Co.
Flat Rock, Carolina Canning Co.
Graham, Curtis Canning Co.
Greensboro, Gilman & Smith.
High Point, High Point C'g Co.
Hobgood, Hobgood Canning Co.
La Grange, Staunton, D. M.
Lexington, Hawes Canning Co.
Lincolnton, Pheifer, Geo. L.
Marion, Marion Canning Co.
Morganton, Gilliam & Shuping.
New Berne, Moore & Brady.
Oliver, W. H.
Newton, Newton Canning Co.
Pittsborough, Womack, J. A.
Rockingham, Stewart C'g Co.
Rutherfordton, Rutherfordton C'g Co.
Salem, Jenkins & Sons.
Salisbury, Lanier, James.
South Washington, McMillan, D. J.
Trenton, Whittaker, T. J.
Warrenton, Bonner, R. L.
Warsaw, Warsaw Canning Co.
Washington, Keenan, J. W.
 McGrath, H. W., & Co.
Willard, Johnson, E. M.

OHIO.

Ada, Peterson, D. S. & H.
Akron, Akron Canning Co.
Albany, Walker, J. E.
Alliance, Alliance Canning Co.
Amelia, Claremont Packing Co.
Beaver, Leest, J. & G.
Belpre, Dana, Geo., & Son.
Chillicothe, McConnell, Clancy & Co.
 Sears & Nichols.
Cincinnati, Challenge Packing Co.
 Clermont Packing Co.
 Fisher Packing Co.
 Skinner & Louden.
 Snider Preserving Co.
Circleville, Sears, C. E., & Co.
Clarksville, Mounts & Van Wirt.
Clyde, Medford Canning Co.
Dayton, Dayton Packing Co.
 Moore, R. W.
Elyray, Elyray Canning Co.
Fremont, Fremont Canning Co.
 Hart, W. H.
 Underwood, E. H.
Huron, Wickham & Co.
Lebanon, Hayner, J. M., P'g Co.
Lima, Lima Canning Co.
Marlborough, Haines Bros. & Co.
Milan, Milan Packing Co.
Morrow, McKinney, W. H.
 Morrow Packing Co.
 South Lebanon Packing Co.
Mt. Washington, Colter P'g Co.
 Kline & Colter.
North Amherst, Amherst P'g Co.
Petersburg, Petersburg C'g Co.
Sabina, McCormick Canning Co.
Salem, McNab, J. B.
 Snook & Co. Packing Co.
Sandusky, Sandusky Canning Co.
South Lebanon, Snook Bros. Packing Co.
 Snook & Sons.
 Snook, W. H.
 South Lebanon Canning Co.
Tiffin, Keppel, W. H.
Toledo, Pliny, Watson & Co.

Urbana, Wagner Bros.
Whitesboro, Whitesboro C'g Co.
Wilmington, McCormick, Lansing & Co.
Winchester, Reese, H. C.
Xenia, Xenia Canning Co.
Zanesville, Spalding, L. P.
    Stern, H. F.

PENNSYLVANIA.

Allentown, Stickle, S. C.
Bryansville, Ruff & Bro. P'g Co.
Delta, Harry, E. W.
    Johnson, C. F.
    Whiteford, J. S.
East Stroudsburg, Van Vliet, J. W.
    Van Vliet, W. R.
Furniss, McSparran, J. G., & Co.
Gettysburg, Gettysburg C'g Co. .
Hanover, Winebrenner, P. F. &
    D. E.
Harrington, Reed, J. C.
Hartsville, Kaisinger, H. W.
Indian Run, Nelson Canning Co.
Lancaster, Leonard, G.
Littletown, Crouse, J. E.
McCall's Ferry, McCall, H. W.
Muddy Creek Forks, Muddy Creek
    Canning Co.
North East, North East C'g Co.
Oxford, Grier, R. J.
Peach Bottom, Barnett & Ramsay.
Philadelphia, Barth, John.
    Beck, Wm. F.
    Levin, S. H., & Sons.
    Levin & Knight.
    Penn Fruit Co.
    Ritter, P. J., Conserve Co.
    Schimmel, J. O., Preserving
    Co.
    Selser Bros. & Co.
    Semple, Matthew & Co.
    Wallace Bros.
    Warner & Rhodes.
Pleasant Grove, Haines Bros.
Riverside, Pitner, Abner.
Stewartstown, Gable, J. B.

Stewartstown, Gable & Son.
    Jordan, J. C.
Wrightsville, McConkey Bros.
York Sulphur Springs, Peters,
    H. C.

RHODE ISLAND.

Providence, Midwood & Sons.
Perry, Francis, H.

SOUTH CAROLINA.

Blackwell, Enterprise C'g Co.
Branchville, Dukes, A. F. H. &
    A. S.
Charleston, McGill, W. J.
Cheraw, Cheraw Canning Co.
Columbia, Brookline C'g Co.
Darlington, Champion C'g Co.
Florence, Florence Canning Co.
Gaffney City, Gaffney City C'g Co.
Graham, Graham Canning Co.
Greenville, Greenville C'g Co.
Lanford Station, Lanford Station
    Canning Co.
Mt. Pleasant, Berkley C'g Co.
Mullins, Hardwick, W. A.
Pendleton, Pendleton C'g Co.
Perry, Sally Canning Co.
Prosperity, Prosperity C'g Co.
Rock Hill, Rock Hill C'g Co.
St. George's, St. George's C'g Co.
West, Westville Canning Co.
White Oak, White Oak C'g Co.
Williamston, Williamston C'g Co.

TENNESSEE.

Apison, Apison Canning Co.
Bristol, Bristol Canning Co.
    Holston Packing Co.
Brownsville, Brownsville C'g Co.
Chattanooga, Chattanooga C'g Co.
Clarksville, Eleazan, Geo.
Cleveland, Cleveland C'g Co.
Curve, Nagle & Harwood.
Dayton, Bolton, R. L.

Dayton, Dayton Canning Co.
Jackson, Sisco, P. G.
Johnson City, Bowman, A. B.
Jonesboro, Dove, J. A.
Marysville, Nebb, A. J.
Morning Star, Deokins, R. W. K.
Nashville, Capital Packing Co.
New Market, New Market C'g Co.
Robinson, B.
Sevierville, McMahon, P. H.

TEXAS.

Alvord, Alvord Canning Co.
Arkansas City, Fulton C'g Co.
Bonham, Bonham Canning Co.
Fulkerson, J. H.
Brownwood, Brownwood C'g Co.
Calvaras, Loyer, G. F.
Clayton, Tinkle, J. F.
Corpus Christi, Royall Givens Packing Co.
Columbus, Guy, J. B.
Dallas, Dallas Canning Co.
Del Rio, Del Rio Canning Co.
Dennison, Dennison Canning Co.
Martin, J. R.
Ennis, Ennis Canning Co.
Fort Worth, Fort Worth C'g Co.
Henderson, Rusk County C'g Co.
Houston, Houston Canning Co.
Jacksonville, Jacksonville C'g Co.
Marshall, Marshall Canning Co.
Mexia, Mexia Canning Co.
Mineola, Mineola Canning Co.
Overton, Overton Canning Co.
Palestine, Ozmant, J. W.
Paris, North Texas Canning Co.
Pilot Point, Pilot Point C'g Co.
Pittsburg, Pittsburg Canning Co.
Sherwood, Sherwood Canning Co.
South Condro, South Condro C'g Co.
Stephenville, Stephenville C'g Co.
Terrell, Terrell Canning Co.
Tyler, East Texas Canning Co.
Long Canning Co.
Tyler Canning Co.

Waco, Waco Canning Co.
Wills Point, Douglass, E.
Wills Point Canning Co.
Wetherford, Wetherford C'g Co.

UTAH.

Ogden, Utah Packing Co.
Salt Lake, Capital Packing Co.

VIRGINIA.

Abingdon, Holston Packing Co.
Kaylor & Hogg.
Somerset Canning Co.
South West Canning Co.
Washington Canning Co.
Alexandria, Alexandria C'g Co.
Alone, Alone Canning Co.
Kirkpatrick, S.
Amherst C. H., Piedmont C'g Co.
Amsterdam, Amsterdam C'g Co.
Atlantic City, Atwood & Co.
Atlees, Hill & Bro.
Black Walnut, Black Walnut C'g Co.
Blue Ridge Springs, Riley Bros.
Bridgewater, Sanger Bros.
Brighton, Ketchum, J. W.
Brugh's Mills, Brugh C'g Co.
Buchannan, Boyd, H. E.
McBreedin, B. F., & Bro.
Carter's Creek, Bussels, J. N., & Co.
Christianburg, Johnson, J. H.
Claremont, Claremont C'g Co.
Cloverdale, Cloverdale C'g Co.
Moomaw, J. C., & Co.
Conyer's Springs, Murray, J. P.
Smiley & Murray.
Weeks & Sons.
Crimora, Crimora Canning Co.
Daleville, Denton & Co.
Neninger, B. F.
Neninger, T. E.
Danville, Danville Canning Co.
Drury's Bluff, Walker, W. T.
Dunsville, Kriete, E. W.

Ellison, Horn, West & Ellison.
Farmville, Farmville Canning Co.
    Venable, A. R.
Fincastle, Crush & Co.
    Figgott & Slicer.
    Holliday, L. P.
    Huff, C. N., & Co.
    Norfsinger & Hoffman.
    Slicer, J. N., & Co.
    Vines, C. H.
Franklin, Gay, J. P.
Front Royal, Front Royal C'g Co.
Galveston, Galveston Canning Co.
Gogginsville, Ikenberry, H.
Grafton, Wade & Sons.
Green Forest, Jordan, J. C., & Co.
Greenway, Greenway Canning Co.
Hague, Hague Canning Co.
Halifax, Halifax Canning Co.
Hamilton, Hoge, J. M.
Harrisonburg, Harrisonburg C'g Co.
Hayes' Store, Rowe, R. A., & Co.
Haymaker's Town, Rice, S. D.
    Ross & Rice.
Hunslett, Tinsley, J. G., & Co.
Kinsale, Courtney & Kline.
    Hardwick, S. B.
Leesburg, Foster, J. W.
Lester Manor, Smith, M. E.
Lexington, Lexington C'g Co.
Lottsburg, Lewis & Sons.
    Turner, C. B.
Lowry, Grabill, Jones & Co.
Luray, Luray Canning Co.
Lynchburg, Cecil Canning Co.
    Urquhart & Co.
Martin's Station, McGill, Jas.
Middletown, Stultz, Fred., & Co.
Natural Bridge, Nair & Burger.
Naylor's, Waddington & Holme.
Norfolk, Perry, N. K., & Co.
Oak Grove, Oak Grove C'g Co.
Oldham, Wright, J. N.
Old Hickory, Booze & Sons.
    Thrasher & Thrasher.
    Williams & Vines.
Pedler's Mills, Woods & Ellis.

Port Royal, Thornton, C. B.
Pulaski City, McGill, J.
Rensens, Booze, J. M.
Rio Vista, Bednock, J. P.
Roanoke, Roanoke Packing Co.
    Virginia Packing Co.
Rustburg, Rustburg Canning Co.
Salem, Garst, H., & Son.
    Garst, J. A., & Co.
    Neninger & Preston.
Saltville, Palmer, G. W.
Spottswood, Spottswood C'g Co.
Stevens City, Baker, D., & Son.
Stockton, Martin, J. H.
Stump, Washington Canning Co.
Suffolk, Singleton Canning Co.
Triford, Evans & Sons.
Trinity, Reynolds, Wm.
    Spigle, Layman & Co.
Troutville, Feather, J. J.
    Kinzey, C. G.
    Kinzey, J. C.
    Layman, A. K.
    Layman, J. G.
    Malls, C. M.
    Shaver, S. L.
    Shoalter, S. C.
Urbana, Gardner & Co.
Vinton, Vinton Canning Co.
Wakema, Lewis, J. W.
Warrenton, Brooks, F.
Waskey's Mills, McCullough & Lewis.
Wythesville, Wythe Canning Co.

WASHINGTON.

Eureka, Eureka Packing Co.

WEST VIRGINIA.

Alderson, Johnson, J. W.
Charleston, Charleston C'g Co.
    Clark, J. P.
Huntington, Crouch, S. G.
Lewisburg, Greenbrier C'g Co.
Wheeling, McMechen, Geo. K., & Son.

WISCONSIN.

Fond du Lac, Level & Hunter.
Milwaukee, Cream City Preserving Co.

Milwaukee, Roundy, Peckham & Co.
Oskosh, Oskosh Packing Co.
Ripon, Ripon Packing Co.

(2.) FISH.

ALASKA.

Afognak, Royal Packing Co.
  Russian-American Salmon Packing Co.
Bartlett Bay, Bartlett Bay Salmon Packing Co.
Bristol Bay, Bristol Bay C'g Co.
Cape Fox, Moira Packing Co.
  Tongass Packing Co.
Cape Lees, Cape Lees Salmon P'g Co.
Chignik, Chignik Bay P'g Co.
  Shumegin Packing Co.
Chilkat, Chilkat Packing Co.
Karluk, Alaska Improvement and Salmon Packing Co.
  Karluk Packing Co.
Kenai, Northern Alaska P'g Co.
Klawack, North-Western P'g Co.
Kodiak, Aleutian Islands P'g Co.
  Hume Packing Co.
  Kodiak Packing Co.
Nushagak, Alaska Packing Co.
Ozernoi, Western Alaska P'g Co.
Prince of Wales Island, Prince of Wales Canning Co.
Prince William's Sound, Pacific Packing Co.
Pyramid Harbor, Pyramid Harbor Packing Co.
Stickeen, Glacier Packing Co.
Tongass, Tongass Canning Co.
Wachusett, Wachusett C'g Co.
Yes Bay, Boston Fishing and Trading Co.

CALIFORNIA.

Colton, Colton Packing Co.
Eel River, Pacific Coast P'g Co.
Requa, Requa Canning Co.

San Francisco, Alaska Salmon Packing & Fur Co.
  Arctic Fishing & P"g Co.
  Astoria Packing Co.
  Booth, A., & Co.
  Bristol Bay Packing Co.
  Central Alaska Co.
  Code, Elfelt & Co.
  Coleman, W. T., & Co.
  Columbus Packing Co.
  Corville, E.
  Cutting Packing Co.
  Dempster & Keys.
  Dodge, Sweeney & Co.
  Hume, G. W.
• Hume, R. D.
  Karluk Packing Co.
  Merrell, N. A.
  Northern Packing Co.
  Nushagak Packing Co.
  Overland Packing Co.
  Pacific Whaling Co.
  Peninsular Trading & Fur Co.
  Sacramento River P'g Co.
  Scotchler & Gibbs.
  Spafford, J. M.
  Star of Columbia Salmon P'g Co.
  Thistle Packing Co.

DELAWARE.

Dover, Chambers, The J. M., P'g Co.

FLORIDA.

Appalachicola, Appalachicola Fish and Oyster Co.
  Appalachicola Canning Co.

10

Appalachicola, Bamburger & Co.
   Rouge Bros.
Bell River, Bell River P'g Co.
Miami, Miami Packing Co.
St. Petersburg, Southern Fish P'g
   Co.
Tampa, Wicks & Bowen.

ILLINOIS.

Chicago, Booth, A., Packing Co.

LOUISIANA.

New Orleans, Booth, A., P'g Co.
   G. W. Dunbar's Sons.
   Gumbel & Co.
   Ranleo, Chas. J.
   Smith Bros. & Co.

MAINE.

Anson, Anson Packing Co.   •
Auburn, Jordan & Collier.
   Potter & Wrightington.
Brooklin, Brooklin Canning Co.
   Holden & McFarland.
   Stephens, S. G.
   Winslow Packing Co.
Cape Elizabeth, Nutter, W. B.
Castine, Castine Packing Co.
Columbia Falls, Columbia Falls
   Packing Co.
Cutler, Kelley Bros.
East La Moine, La Moine C'g Co.
Eastport, American Sardine Co.
   Balcom, Wm.
   Blanchard, H., & Sons.
   Capen, G. W.
   Eagle Preserve Fish Co.
   Goodey, Geo., & Co.
   Green, Roberts & Co.
   Hallett Bros.
   Henderson, John.
   Holmes, E. A.
   Holmes, M. C., & Co.
   Judson & Young.

Eastport, Kemp, N. H.
   McCullough, D.
   McLean, A.
   O'Grady, G., & Co.
   Quoddy Packing Co.
   Raye, Geo. F., & Co.
Green's Landing, Thurlow,
   Knowlton & Co.
Hurricane Island, Hurricane
   Island Canning Co.
Jonesport, Smith, Rieney & Co.
   Underwood & Co.
Lubec, Avery, E. & W.
   Brown, E. W., & Co.
   Comstock, H., & Co.
   Lawrence Packing Co.
   Lubec Packing Co.
   New England Sardine Co.
   Quoddy Packing Co.
Machiasport, Buck's Harbor P'g
   Co.
   Indian Cove Packing Co.
   Machiasport Packing Co.
   Millbridge Packing Co.
Millbridge, Wyman, J. & E. A.
Monmouth, Monmouth C'g Co.
Newport, Newport Canning Co.
North Berwick, Plummer, J. P.
   & D.
Portland, Burnham & Morrill.
   Portland Packing Co.
   Shaw, Hammond & Kearney.
Robinston, Frontier Sardine P'g
   Co.
   Wentworth & Co.
Sedgwick, Gott, Young & Co.
South Freeport, Lewis Bros.
South-West Harbor, Lawton Bros.
South Lubec, Sanders, J. W.
Swan's Island, Castine P'g Co.
Tremont, Bar Harbor P'g Co.
West Pembroke, Pembroke Pack-
   ing Co.
   Pembroke Sardine Co.
Yarmouth, Yarmouth P'g Co.

MARYLAND.

Baltimore, Aughinbaugh C'g Co.
Beckwith, H.
Booth, A., Packing Co.
Boyer, W. W., & Co.
Ellis, W. L., & Co.
Farren, J. S., & Co.
Fait & Winebrenner.
Fleming & Co.
Foote, D. E.
Freeman & Shaw.
Gibbs Preserving Co.
Grebb, L.
Grecht, W., & Co.
Hemingway, H. F.
Houghton Packing Co.
McGrath, H. W., & Co.
Mallory, E. B., & Co.
Miller Bros. & Co.
Moore & Brady.
Myer, T. J., & Co.
Neubert, Chas.
Neubert, Jno. A.
Pearson, C. H., & Co.
Platt & Co.
Underhill, J. J.
Wagner, The Martin, Co.
Winebrenner, P. F. & D. E.
Oxford, Crab Packing Co.

MASSACHUSETTS.

Boston, Bell, W. G., & Co.
Knight & McIntyre.
New England Preserving Co.
Pickert, L., & Co.
Potter & Wrightington.
Spurr, H. B., & Co.
Underwood, W.
Orleans, Bailey Canning & Preserving Co.

MICHIGAN.

Detroit, Hamblin, J. G.

MISSISSIPPI.

Biloxi, Barataria Canning Co.
Biloxi Canning Co.
Biloxi, Gorenflo, Wm., & Co.
Hitchcock, H. W.
Joullian, E. C.
Lopez, Dunbar's Sons & Co.
Maybury, J. T.
Sea Coast Packing Co.

NEW YORK.

Long Island City, Bridge & Gregory.
Myer & Lange.

OREGON.

Astoria, Astoria Packing Co.
Badollet & Co.
Booth, A., Packing Co.
British America Packing Co.
Chilkat Packing Co.
Columbia Canning Co.
Columbia River Packing Co.
Devlin, J. A., & Co.
Ellmore, Sam'l.
Fishermen's Packing Co.
George & Baker.
Gibson, Quackenbush & Co.
Hawthorn, J. O., & Co.
Hume, G. W.
I. X. L. Packing Co.
Morgan, D., Jr.
Occident Packing Co.
Nehalem Packing Co.
Pacific Union Packing Co.
Smith, G. G., & Co.
Union Packing Co.
Williams, J., & Co.
Washington Packing Co.
Clifton, Oregon Packing Co.
Dalles, Evording & Ferrell.
Ellensburg, Hume, R. D.
Gardner, Bath Canning Co.
Gloucester, Gloucester P'g Co.
Oregon City Packing Co.
Lower Cascades, Warren P'g Co.
Oregon City, Logus & Dieringer.
Lovejoy, Mrs. A. L.
Portland, Columbia Canning Co.
Cook, J. W. & V.
George & Baker.

Portland, Hapgood & Co.
　McGowan, P. J., & Co.
　Smith, W. D., & Co.
　The Dalles C'g & P'g Co.
　Warren Packing Co.
Pillar Rock, Pillar Rock C'g Co.
Randolph, Mt. Hood Packing Co.

SOUTH CAROLINA.

Annandale, Hazzard, Wm. M.
Charleston, Edisto Fish & Oyster
　Packing Co.

TEXAS.

Corpus Christi, Givens Oyster C'g
　Co.

VIRGINIA.

Hampton, Gilbert, A. J., & Co.
　McMenamin & Co.

Norfolk, Chamberlain & Co.
　Maltby, Barnes & Co.
　Perry & Co.
　Perry & Johnson.
　Thomas, T. R., & Co.
　Vermillion, J.
Portsmouth, Dutton, W. C.

WASHINGTON.

Aberdeen, Aberdeen Packing Co.
　Pacific Salmon Packing Co.
　Washingtonian Packing Co.
Brookfield, Pillar Rock C'g Co.
Cape Horn, Hapgood & Co.
Chinook, McGowan, P. J., & Co.
Eureka, Eureka Packing Co.
Knappton, Knappton Packing Co.
　North Shore Packing Co.
Milton, Puget Sound Packing Co.
Montesano, Montesano P'g Co.
Seattle, Morse Canning Co.

(3.) MEATS.

CALIFORNIA.

Benicia, Carquinez Packing Co.
San Francisco, Armour P'g Co.
　Columbus Packing Co.
　Cutting Packing Co.
　Goetsen, Nicholas.
　King Morse Canning Co.
　Merry, Faull & Co.
　Schammel Packing Co.
　Wilson, J. Y.

CONNECTICUT.

New London, Pequot Preser'g Co.

DELAWARE.

Dover, Chambers, The J. M., P'g Co.
　Richardson & Robbins.
Frederika, Reynolds & Postels.

ILLINOIS.

Chicago, Armour Packing Co.
　Booth, A., Packing Co.
　Delafield, Morgan & Kissell.

Chicago, Fairbank Canning Co.
　Libby, McNeil & Libby.
　Reiber Preserving Co.

INDIANA.

Kokoma, Brookside Canning Co.

MICHIGAN.

Ann Arbor, Almendring &
　Schneider.

MISSOURI.

Kansas City, Anglo-American P'g
　Co.
　Armour Packing Co.
　Hurst Packing Co.
　Klock & Downing.

OHIO.

Cincinnati, Challenge Packing Co.
　Clermont Packing Co.
　Colter Packing Co.
　Fisher, A., Manufacturing Co.
　Verhage, Henry, Preser'g Co.

INDEX.

149

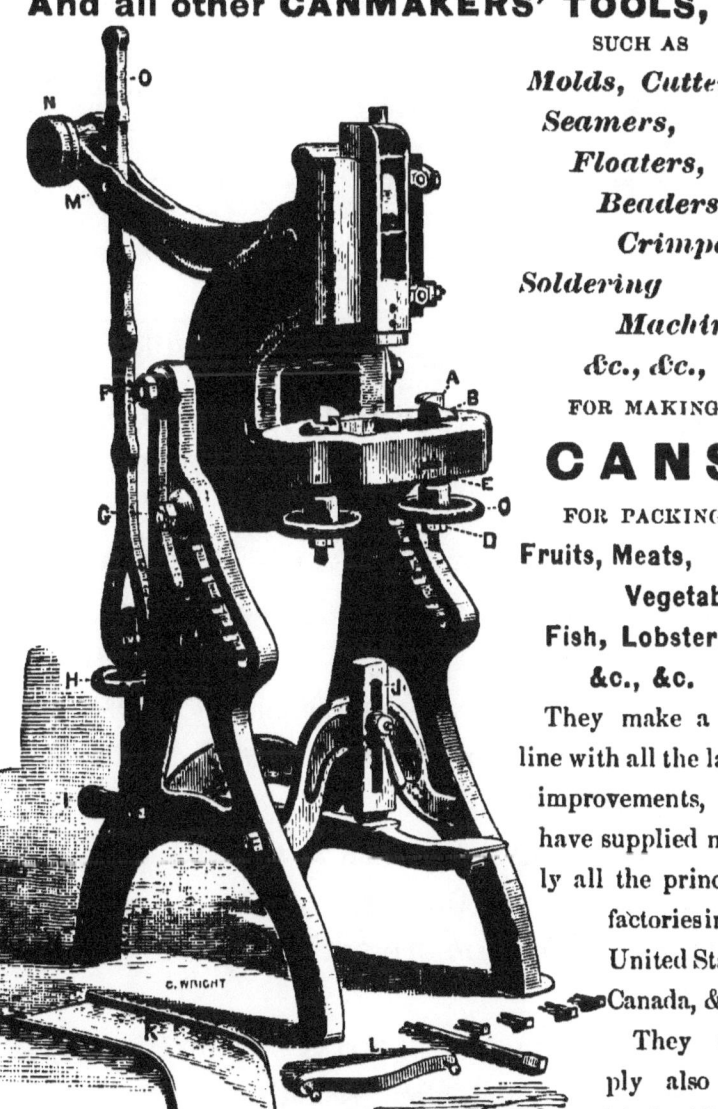

NORTON BROTHERS,

36 to 46 River Street,

CHICAGO,

MANUFACTURERS OF

FRUIT CANS

AND

SOLDER HEMMED CAPS.

The Cans made wholly by machinery under the NOR-TON SYSTEM of AUTOMATIC MACHINES are in every way superior to those made by hand or by any other process. The four great factories operating this system in Chicago, New York, San Francisco, and Hamilton, Canada, have a capacity of

ONE MILLION CANS PER DAY,

and this product is rapidly superseding all other styles of Cans.

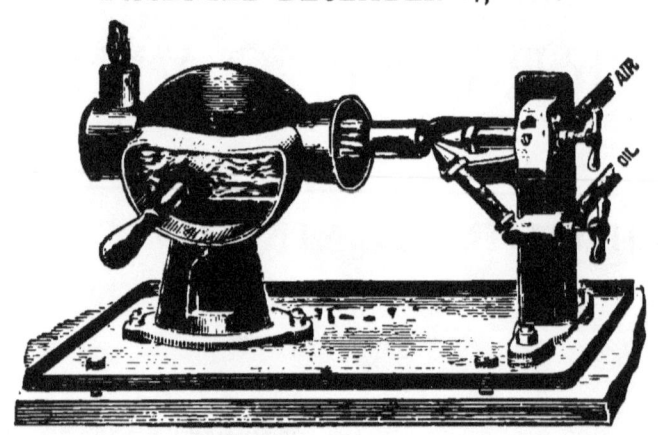

W. S. KNIGHT & CO.,

COMMISSION MERCHANTS,

AND

BROKERS

IN

CANNED GOODS,

No. 43 South Water Street,

CHICAGO.

CORRESPONDENCE SOLICITED